"This isn't Laura. I don't know whose body it is, but it isn't my sister's."

Deputy Steve Gardner's brow wrinkled, and he looked as if he wanted to say all kinds of things. Instead he stood there silently for a moment before he asked a simple question. "Why do you say that?"

"She had a tattoo on her ankle." Jessie pointed to the leg of the mostly burned body on the bed. The pale skin of her ankle was unmarked by fire or anything else. Who had just died in this hospital room? And where was her sister, Laura?

"How sure are you that this isn't your sister?" Steve asked.

"I'm positive, but I feel so confused. Whoever this was, she must have looked a lot like Laura before all this happened to her." Her eyes widened and she sat down quickly.

"What is it?"

"I know it's not Laura, but I just realized something. The one time this woman spoke to me, she called me by name."

Books by Lynn Bulock

Love Inspired Suspense

Where Truth Lies #56
No Love Lost #59
To Trust a Stranger #69

Love Inspired

Gifts of Grace #80
Looking for Miracles #97
Walls of Jericho #125
The Prodigal's Return #144
Change of the Heart #181
The Harbor of His Arms #204
Protecting Holly #279

Steeple Hill Single Title

Love the Sinner
Less Than Frank

LYNN BULOCK

has been writing since fourth grade and has been a published author in various fields for over twenty years. Her first romantic novel came out in 1989 and has been followed by more than twenty books since then. She lives near Los Angeles, California, with her husband. They have two grown sons.

To Trust a Stranger
LYNN BULOCK

Steeple Hill®

Published by Steeple Hill Books™

STEEPLE HILL BOOKS

Steeple
Hill®

ISBN-13: 978-0-373-44259-1
ISBN-10:   0-373-44259-9

TO TRUST A STRANGER

Copyright © 2007 by Lynn M. Bulock

www.SteepleHill.com

Printed in U.S.A.

I will say of the LORD, "He is my refuge and my fortress, my God, in whom I trust."
—*Psalms* 91:2

To Joe, always

And

To Cheryl, my friend and encourager

PROLOGUE

Twenty-four years ago

Jessie Barker sat in the backseat of her parents' car, staying as quiet as possible. Mouse quiet. Falling-leaf quiet. So quiet they wouldn't hear her breathing and know she was awake while they had another argument.

As the station wagon rolled along the dark country road Mommy and Daddy were arguing in the front seat. In the backseat Jessie curled up against the door as much as she could with her seat belt still on and pretended to be anyplace else besides where she was. She looked through slitted eyes at her little sister, Laura, sitting next to her. Laura just looked down at the floor, but then Laura was brave, or maybe too young to understand.

Jessie wanted to yell back at Mommy and Daddy

and tell them how to do their job. If she was a mom she would never yell at her kids and she'd let them watch cartoons on TV, and sometimes she would buy the good kinds of cereal from the store, the ones with marshmallows. Then Jessie and her kids would eat it straight out of the box. Mommy never bought the marshmallow kind of cereal because she didn't like it.

They were still yelling in the front seat. It was the same thing again. This time it went on so long that Laura finally leaned over and whispered to Jessie. "Why doesn't she just try it? They make us try at least three bites of everything at the dinner table, even gross, slimy asparagus."

Jessie knew she looked at her sister as if she was stupid. Jessie felt bad when she did that, but she couldn't help it. She looked at Laura a lot that way. "Try what?"

"The tea. The fackle tea. Daddy said if Mommy was the right kind of fackle tea wife we could stay here for ten years. That's a long time."

Jessie sighed. "There's no tea, Laura. That is *not* what he means. You are so dumb."

"It's still a long time," Laura said. She turned her face toward the other door so Jessie wouldn't see her cry. Jessie ignored her as she spread her fingers out in front of her, looking at the little bit of Hot-Hot

Pink nail polish she put on her right pointer finger yesterday before Mommy caught her and made her stop. Laura was right about one thing. Ten years was a long time. If they could stay in the nice apartment they had now for ten years, maybe Laura could go to Jessie's school when she was old enough to start kindergarten in the fall.

"And I still don't see why we had to take this route—" Jessie could hear Daddy mutter "—middle of nowhere."

Did nowhere have a middle? If you were nowhere, how did you know when you got to the middle of it? Jessie wanted to ask somebody about that, but her parents were still fighting so she kept quiet. Jessie was still thinking about the middle of nowhere when she really drifted off to sleep.

That was when the bang came.

The loud noise startled Jessie awake. She felt hot and sweaty and didn't know where she was. Rough hands pulled her out of the car, making her cry out because they didn't unhook her seat belt first, only unfastening it when she yelled. Where were they? What was happening?

It was dark and scary and she couldn't see anybody else at first, not even Laura. Once she was out in the night air she wasn't hot for very long; she only had a sweater on instead of a coat and the wind was cold. Then Laura started to whimper. Jessie spied a patch of tall weeds and pulled Laura close to her into it, feeling the need to hide. "Be quiet," Jessie whispered.

When her eyes got used to the dark Jessie could see some more things. A strange man was talking to Mommy. The man was big and loud and he looked mean. Laura shrank away from the noise and for once Jessie just hugged her and patted her. She couldn't see Daddy anyplace, and nobody was paying any attention to two little kids, even the other man who had dumped her out of the car. Laura cried without a sound, shivering in Jessie's arms.

After a while Laura struggled free and she called out softly, even though Jessie dragged her back even farther in the weeds. "Mommy? Daddy?" Nobody noticed either of them. Jessie couldn't see much of what was going on.

The big man said something else and Mommy started screaming louder than she had been when she and Daddy were arguing in the front seat. "No. Not the babies. That wasn't the way it was supposed to go." What babies? Did they mean her and Laura? Jessie was a first-grader and her sister was almost five. Neither of them were *babies*.

The big man standing with Mommy looked mad.

"What are we supposed to do? We can't take them. You want us to leave 'em on the side of the road?"

Mommy stopped screaming. "Yes. I do." She looked at Jessie but something about the look on her mother's face made her stand still where she was instead of running to Mommy the way she felt like doing. Jessie had let go of her sister but Laura wasn't moving, either.

Why didn't Daddy get out of the car and check on them? Daddy was always the one who checked when Laura had a fever or Jessie skinned her knee or anything. Mommy looked worried sometimes, but Daddy gave the hugs and said "It will be all right" when he was home.

Laura looked as though she could use a hug right now. She was crying harder, and her nose was running. Jessie was just trying to stay as quiet as she'd been in the car. Something told her that making noise would be a very bad thing right now. Jessie grabbed Laura's hand again and she could feel her sister trembling.

The big man who was the boss, the one dressed in black with a leather jacket, was saying things to the other men. One of them walked over and shoved the girls roughly far away from the car and Laura sat down hard in the rocks and grass by the side of the road. The big man took Mommy by the arm and said, "Come on. Let's go." She didn't even look back at the girls. Laura started to wail then. Jessie tried to cover her mouth, but it didn't matter. Nobody paid attention to either of them.

The big man and Mommy got in another car, a big black one. They drove away. Where were they going? Did they really mean to leave them here all alone?

Jessie started to run toward Daddy's car, hoping that he would help them. She stopped after taking only a few steps. A man was dragging a lady across the ground. She looked funny, all limp, and she wasn't moving. He stuffed her in the front seat of the car where Mommy usually sat and slammed the door. Jessie could see Daddy still sitting behind the wheel but he didn't look right, either. He wasn't moving and he slumped over toward the middle of the car.

Then the other men did something to Daddy's car and it rolled down a hill. There was a loud noise and fire and then the men got into the other car and it drove away. Daddy never came back. Laura cried so hard she threw up.

For a long time it was just the two of them out in the dark. Then the fire truck and the police cars came and there was a lot of noise. Nobody would believe Jessie about Mommy and the big man in the black car. And through it all, Laura just howled.

No matter how many times Jessie told the story in the coming days through the hospital and the offices and the foster homes, nobody ever believed her. The grown-ups in charge acted as if she was making stuff up. One of them even told her that she had to face the fact that Mommy and Daddy died in the car accident and act like a big girl about it.

It all made Jessie want to quit talking altogether, as Laura had done. After she quit howling in the dark, it was four days before Jessie heard her sister talk again. By the time she did, she wanted to talk to Jessie about what they'd seen and heard. By then all Jessie would tell her was "Forget it ever happened." If nobody believed her, why should she keep telling the same story? Jessie was only six, but already she had learned that the world was a dark and scary place and there was nobody in it who wanted to help her.

ONE

"He's late," Jessie Barker said to her sister. "You said he was going to be here by eleven."

"Well, he isn't here, is he?" Laura rolled her eyes the same way she had when they were kids. "Not everybody can be as punctual as you. Maybe his car broke down, or the traffic is backed up on the bridge, or he overslept or something."

Jessie sniffed. "Those are all excuses I don't let my students get away with. Why should I take them from a Web site designer?"

"Because he's willing to work cheap and give us a decent product. And stop shaking your head at me like that, unless you want to hear my opinion on your hair color."

"I don't. I like my brown just the way it is. And I don't see why a beautician needs a Web site."

Laura sighed in her dramatic way. "Esthetician,

sweetie. I'm not a beautician. Leave it to you to look down your nose at my business *and* get things wrong at the same time."

Her attitude made Jessie want to stick her tongue out at her sister. Why did they always argue like this? Probably because neither of them had anyone else to turn to. Laura wasn't ready to let it go yet. "Having my own Web site would be a great help for my business. I could link it to the day spa's site and get more clients. Besides, I figure I could interest some people with a few beauty hints. That would reach a lot more women on the Web than a newspaper ad." Unable to sit still while she talked, Laura dusted the coffee table.

"So the print medium is worthless now?" Jessie looked over her glasses at Laura, who looked as though she could feel a headache coming on.

"Nuts, Jessie. Why do you always make me feel like I've said the wrong thing? I'm twenty-nine years old and around you I still feel like a kid. And not a very smart one, either."

Jessie melted a little. She always did when Laura looked hurt. "I'm sorry. I didn't mean to growl at you, but you hit a nerve with that newspapers-are-worthless comment."

Laura waved a hand. "Now I didn't say they were worthless. You know I wouldn't ever say that. In fact, I thought you'd want a Web site to promote your new book and link to online bookstores. It would sell a lot more copies that way, wouldn't it?"

Jessie shrugged. Laura might not have been labeled the "smart one" when they were kids, but she'd always been creative. "If you think that many people would be interested in a history of urban legends published by a small university press."

Her sister's face lit up, showing how beautiful she was. "Of course I do. You could probably get a spot on the radio or even get interviewed by one of the TV features reporters just by promoting your book on the Web."

It sounded good, but first things first, Jessie thought. "If you say so. But to do that I'd have to have a Web site. And to have a Web site your Web designer would have to *show up*, now wouldn't he?"

Laura pressed one hand to her temple. "Couldn't you be something other than logical and literal just once in your life?" Then she laughed. "No, probably not. You wouldn't be Jessie then."

Before Jessie could respond, Laura was grabbing her purse. "Look, if it's such a big deal I'll go looking for him, okay? Give him a break, anyway. He's not a whole lot older than most of your students. He probably just overslept or something. Computer geeks keep odd hours."

Jessie tried to still the aggravation she felt. "I'm not all that familiar with them. They don't speak up in class." Not even in the "pop culture" class that was her favorite, where she got a lot of responses from most of the students.

Laura grabbed her car keys and headed for the garage. She called over her shoulder to her sister. "I'll call you if there's any kind of problem. Otherwise I'll be back here, probably with Adrian in tow, in the next hour, okay?"

"Fine." Jessie tried to look interested in a stack of papers she had to grade. Anything so that Laura didn't see the look of worry she knew crossed her face as her sister left. Laura was an adult. There was no sense in treating her like a child.

Cassidy stood in the shadows across the street from Adrian's town house and watched as Laura Barker knocked on the door. To Cassidy, Laura looked more like a teenager than a woman in her late twenties, with her bouncy step and the way she rapped on the door. When the door opened, the man answering looked far older than Laura Barker, mature and wary in a way Laura wasn't, even though he was years younger.

After Laura went inside, Cassidy pondered how much time to give the two together. It all depended on how much Adrian Bando had connected the dots with the information he had. Cassidy knew the young man was bright; if he'd worked things through and now shared that information with Laura, everything could fall apart even after all these years of careful concealment.

Cassidy knew that timing could be everything. One wrong decision made life collapse like a row of dominoes. Suddenly there was another figure at the door and Cassidy scrambled for even more cover. Being seen now was a bad idea. The figure at the door stood impatiently, checking the street. Then he made a quick motion at the lock, and the door opened without anyone on the other side. Half a block away the noise of an idling engine stopped. The driver of a black sedan opened the door and stepped from the car.

Fifteen minutes later the driver slipped back behind the wheel of the car. The engine purred to life and he pulled away from the curb, slowly turning the corner to disappear from view. If the town house had a back door onto the alley behind it, the car could stop there without being seen.

Ten minutes later Cassidy stood at the front door of the town house, listening for clues to the situation. It was too quiet for more than one person to be in the place. The woman Cassidy found was surprisingly still alive. In fact, if anybody came to her aid now, she might live. That would mess up everything, Cassidy thought. But it was easy to fix.

Thirty minutes later an unidentified person made a 911 call from the pay phone across the street from the town house. By then the fire had been burning long enough that the woman inside would be no trouble to anyone. In the chaos of the arriving fire trucks, no one paid any attention to the nondescript person in jeans walking away from the complex.

Where was her sister? Jessie was at the pacing stage. Laura was usually really good at calling if she was going to be late. Of course she wasn't quite as good at remembering to charge her cell phone, so she might have had the best of intentions and not followed through. That was Laura. Still, most of the time she showed up when and where she said she would.

Living with Laura's quirks and habits was such a part of her life Jessie knew them all by heart. And they hadn't changed that much since Jessie's junior year in college. That was when Laura had turned eighteen and aged out of foster care. At the ripe old age of twenty Jessie gave up her brief taste of the carefree life on campus to find an apartment for the two of them and make a home for them.

Even that long ago it had been Laura who'd concerned herself with the niceties of things. Jessie would have been content with "starving student" decor like bookshelves from planks and cinder blocks and a couple of mattresses on the floor if she had to have it that way. Their finances didn't allow for much more. Still, Laura was always filling a jelly glass with wildflowers, or scrounging around in thrift stores for something else to give the place a little lift.

The doorbell rang, jarring Jessie out of her thoughts. "Finally." She went to the condo's incredibly small front hall and looked through the peephole. The man on the other side of the door was alone and he didn't look the way Laura had described the Web designer. Maybe he had gotten a haircut for the occasion.

"Adrian?" she asked, opening the door.

"No, I'm afraid not. Were you expecting him?" In the light of day it was easy to see this definitely wasn't Adrian. This man was taller, lean in a fit way and his hair was a lighter brown than Laura's description.

Laura had called Adrian sort of different looking. "He has long black hair, usually tied back, and he's very pale. Looks like the black belt martial artist that he is, somebody you wouldn't want to meet in a dark alley. But so far he's been this big teddy bear to me."

This man was older than her students, probably older than her for that matter. Sharply dressed in a dark suit, the set of his jaw said he was definitely no teddy bear. He'd asked her a question and Jessie wasn't sure how much information she should give a stranger, no matter how good-looking or nicely dressed he was. She decided to go with the minimum. "Yes, I was expecting someone. We had an eleven o'clock appointment."

"If it's Adrian Bando, he won't be keeping it. I'm Stephen Gardner with the St. Charles County sheriff's department. I'm looking for Jessica Barker."

"I'm Jessica. And I'd like some proof you're with the sheriff's department." He nodded and took out his identification as if he expected it. She looked it over quickly, trying not to panic. "Nobody who knows me calls me Jessica except for something very official. What's wrong?"

The man on the doorstep shook his head slowly, looking even more serious than before. "If you don't mind, let's do this inside." He looked like Jessie knew she did when she had to tell a kid they were on academic probation. So the news wouldn't be good. She asked him in then because she was afraid that if she stood there in the doorway talking to Stephen Gardner any longer she might pass out.

"Something's happened to Laura, hasn't it?" Jessie didn't usually get flustered easily but there was an air about Gardner that sounded alarms in her head. "Tell me she's not dead."

He looked a little relieved then but his dark eyes were still somber. "She's not dead, Ms. Barker. But she is in Mercy Hospital thanks to Adrian Bando or somebody who was in his apartment. And it's bad. Quite bad."

Jessie felt her heart in her throat. "How bad? Are you saying she might not make it? She's only been gone a little while. What on earth happened?"

"There was a fire. And something happened to your sister even before that. I don't think the doctors know yet how serious her other injuries are. But I know we need to hurry. If you get your things I can take you to the hospital."

Jessie got ready faster than she'd ever done anything in her life. Only halfway to the hospital in the unmarked sheriff's department sedan did she notice that she wore two different tennis shoes. She hoped against hope that once she got to the hospital she could laugh with Laura about the shoes. Then she worried the rest of the way there that she might not get the chance.

TWO

Was this her sister? Jessie knew the still figure on the hospital bed had to be Laura, but her brain couldn't process what she was seeing. The woman on the bed could have been anybody the same height and weight as her sister. The one eye not swollen shut was the same bright blue as Laura's, but it wasn't focused. Most of her hair was gone, burned in the fire that consumed far too many other things for Jessie to hope that her sister would live. But the hair that was left was the same dark gold Jessie knew. She'd envied it for years, knowledge that sent pain knifing through her now.

"Her lungs filled with smoke from the fire. That's why she's on the ventilator, and partially sedated so that she doesn't fight the machines," the nurse explained softly.

"Is there anyplace that I can touch her? Can I hold

her hand?" Tears blurred Jessie's vision and clogged her throat. It was hard to find a patch of skin on her sister that wasn't burned, bandaged or had medical equipment attached.

"You can sit here next to her. She's going to drift in and out some, given the amount of pain medication she's on. If she gets more lucid she'll probably be glad to see a familiar face." Jessie nodded numbly and found the hard plastic chair, pulling it as close to the bed as she could without getting in the way of anything attached to Laura.

At least she wasn't alone. The man from the sheriff's department was still there, just outside the cubicle. "How did you know who she was, or how to get in touch with me?" she asked him. What was his title, anyway? In all the upheaval she didn't remember any of that, if he'd even told her. Was he a deputy or a detective, or something else altogether?

His voice sounded only a little less choked than hers. "Her purse was in the entryway of the apartment on the floor. It apparently wasn't a robbery, because her money and credit cards were there along with her driver's license."

Her sister had hated her last driver's license photo, Jessie remembered. Laura said it made her look "goofy." Staring down at the puffy, unfamiliar face Jessie ached. What she wouldn't give right now for her sister to look merely goofy.

"There was one more thing. What does this mean to you?" Gardner held out a snapshot, faded and worn with one corner ripped off.

"That's us," Jessie said, wondering why on earth Laura had it with her. The two little girls smiled out at the camera, sitting on a blanket in the park. Memories rushed in as she saw the image. She could almost feel the hot sun on her shoulders and taste the tart lemonade they'd taken on the picnic. "It's the only picture we managed to keep of the two of us before…our parents died." There was no sense in getting into their tangled history with this man. Better to just stick to the official version that everyone else insisted was the truth anyway.

"You must have been awfully young when that happened." Jessie didn't know when she'd heard such compassion in someone's voice without pity. In the short time she'd known him, this man struck her as unique. She only wished she'd met him under different circumstances.

"I was six and Laura was four. The picture was taken about a month before the accident."

He looked at the photo again. "Can you think of any reason for your sister to have this with her?"

Jessie shook her head, listening to the machines

whoosh and beep around them. "Not really. Maybe later she can explain that."

His pained silence said more than words would have. *He didn't think there was going to be a later for Laura.* And looking at the still figure in front of her, Jessie was afraid he might be right.

"What do I call you, anyway?" It had been hours since she and Steve Gardner had really conversed. He'd gotten them bad coffee from a vending machine or the hospital cafeteria, and a couple of apples. Even though she was hungry, Jessie couldn't imagine eating much else with the trauma going on around her. She was still hoping that someone would come out of Laura's cubicle and tell them that things were dramatically better; that she'd turned the corner and then Jessie would go eat something.

That hope was starting to fade, but Jessie tried to keep it alive even in the face of the gravity of the situation. Several cubicles in the unit were filled with people, and a full complement of doctors and nurses attending to them. Laura hadn't shown any clarity or recognition yet.

The officer tossed a mostly empty coffee cup into the waste can in the corner of the family lounge. Hospital staff had shooed them out of Laura's cubicle and hadn't let them back in yet. "What do you mean?"

"Your title. It's obviously not just plain 'Mr.' Gardner. Are you a deputy, a detective, what?"

"Technically I'm a deputy, and also an investigator. I've passed the test for detective but haven't gotten the promotion officially yet." He looked as tired as Jessie felt. She watched him reach up and try to knead a knot out of his neck. In this windowless room, Jessie realized she had no idea what time of day it was.

Looking down at her watch for the first time in a long while, Jessie felt shock. They'd been at the hospital over seven hours. "You probably were off duty hours ago, weren't you?"

The deputy shrugged. "In a case like this, it doesn't matter. Besides, I brought you here. If I leave now, how will you get back home?"

"I won't be going home for a while. Not until I talk to my sister, or…" Jessie couldn't force herself to finish her sentence.

"Or she is past the point of talking," Deputy Gardner finished. "I'm likely to stay until then, too."

"You don't think she's going to make it, do you?" Jessie challenged.

His dark eyes flashed. "I'm not a doctor, so I can't predict what will happen. But I'll admit that things don't look good. If she makes it, she'll be in the hospital a long time. You realize that, don't you?"

Jessie nodded. She felt the same way, but she couldn't think about saying goodbye to her sister. Laura was the only family she had. What would happen if she died? "I just wish there was something I could do."

"Other than pray I don't think there's anything that anybody, including most of the doctors, can do for her right now."

"Pray? Do you really think that helps anybody?" Did someone like this man who saw all the evil in life really believe in prayer? It sounded as likely as one of the urban legends she researched.

"I think it helps." The deputy's face held no hint of a smile. "Many times I think it's the only thing that helps."

"Suit yourself. I can't imagine something like that helping."

He looked at her silently and lifted one shoulder, seeming to wordlessly indicate that he wasn't going to argue with her. That was good. There didn't seem to be anybody else on her side except this deputy. This wasn't the time for them to pick a fight.

Deputy Gardner finally went home in the early hours of the morning. He tried one more time to get Jessie to let him take her home. "They'll call you if anything changes. You need some rest," he argued.

Her temper flared. "How do you know what I need? It isn't your sister in the intensive care unit." Jessie regretted her words the moment she said them. This man had stayed with her at the hospital for hours and here she was snarling at him.

It made her feel even worse when he seemed to be fighting tears. He brushed the back of one hand over his eyes and sighed. "You're right. I'm sorry I suggested it. But I've been up for about twenty hours and I have to go home and get some sleep and a shower. I just thought you might want to do the same."

Jessie tried to keep calm. "Honestly, thank you for your concern but I'll stay. I'm afraid that if they called me I wouldn't have time to get back here."

He nodded. "It could be a possibility. Is there anything I can bring you when I come back?"

Her mind felt totally blank. "Maybe breakfast that didn't come from a vending machine. And a roll of quarters or a cell phone charger."

"I think I'll go for the quarters. There isn't anyplace on this floor that we're supposed to use a cell phone." Jessie felt grateful that he understood that much. She didn't want to get any farther from Laura than she had to. Even the nurses were beginning to point out problems that Laura was experiencing. Jessie knew that wasn't a good sign. After midnight a doctor had been in to examine her, and then told them solemnly that they wouldn't be preparing her for debriding and skin graft surgery in the morning.

That was when Jessie knew she was waiting out a vigil that would only last a day or so…perhaps a lot less. "Maybe you should just go into work instead of coming back here. Start trying to find out who did this to my sister," she blurted with more anger than she expected.

"There are folks doing that already. We've got fire inspectors and crime scene investigators sifting through everything at Bando's apartment. Until they're done we can't do much else."

"Okay, then. I'll see you later."

"Try to get some sleep. I know they'll wake you up if you sleep in the family waiting room." Jessie remembered seeing several recliners tucked into corners there and she could almost hear one calling her name.

"I'll get some rest, as much as I can." Jessie didn't expect to sleep with everything going on, but was surprised how quickly exhaustion claimed her when she pulled a soft blanket over her in the vinyl chair.

It only felt like a few minutes later that someone was shaking her awake. "Ms. Barker? Laura's more alert. And the doctor wants to let her off the ventilator soon so that she can talk a little if she's able."

Jessie came out of the blur of sleep, sitting up in the darkened room. The clock on the wall announced that someone had pulled the shades to block the morning sun. She felt thankful that the other families had vacated the room and let her sleep into daylight hours. She tried to digest the nurse's words. Did taking Laura off the ventilator mean she was rallying or that this was a last time to talk?

"Is Deputy Gardner back? Or should you call him?"

"He's on the way," the young nurse said. "Now why don't we find you a cup of coffee and a little time to wash up and you can go see your sister."

Jessie took a few minutes to pull herself together. She tried to avoid really looking in the mirror, knowing she wouldn't like what she saw. She felt haggard and haunted and knew from experience there would be circles under her eyes. Splashing cool water on her face, she found a comb in her purse and ran it through her hair.

Then she remembered who she would be seeing. This was her beautiful sister who was always after her to take better care of herself. Drawing a shaky breath, Jessie forced herself to do her hair with more attention and found a tube of lipstick in the bottom of her purse. She willed her hand not to shake as she put it on, and then went in to see Laura.

Jessie stifled a gasp when she saw her sister. Laura seemed to have gone downhill rapidly in the five hours or so that she'd been sleeping. Her face was even puffier than before, and bruises of all colors streaked everywhere. Still, there was a little more focus to her one good eye. Jessie saw that the head of Laura's bed was raised so that she was lifted into a better position to breathe or speak.

The nurse who'd gotten Jessie from the family lounge positioned herself there, leaning over. "Laura? We're going to take you off the ventilator like we talked about. You may not be able to stay off of it long, but this will give you a chance to talk to your sister."

Then the nurse looked at Jessie. "I'm going to have to ask you to step to the doorway for just a moment so that we can take the breathing tube out. I'll call you back in less than a minute."

Jessie nodded, too upset to speak right now without letting Laura hear the panic she felt. She stepped to the other side of the curtain that made up the front wall of Laura's cubicle. Outside Deputy Gardner was there again.

He didn't look much more rested than she did. His hair was slicked back as if still wet from the shower and his blue shirt and red tie looked hastily put on. "Ms. Barker. They paged me at home. Are things worse?"

"It looks like it. They're taking her off the ventilator so that she can talk." Jessie felt her eyes fill with tears. "Do you want to speak to her first? I know you need to ask her questions about who did this."

The investigator shook his head. "You need to talk to her before I do. She's on enough pain medication that she may not be able to answer my questions anyway. Plus, she'll probably panic if she sees a stranger first. When you've had a chance to talk, maybe I'll come in."

Jessie appreciated his kindness, but she knew that there might not be much time. She wanted him to get as much information as he could, to find out who had done this to her sister.

"You can come in with me now. I'll tell her who you are. And after we've had a chance to talk I'll let you have your time." It was important that Laura talked to the deputy in case she could identify her attacker.

The nurse motioned them back in and Jessie went to the head of Laura's bed, sitting in the chair next to her and making herself stay dry-eyed. "Hi, sweetie. It's me. I'll stay here as long as you want me to." Her sister's hand reached out and grasped hers with surprising strength. "And the man with me here is Deputy Steve Gardner. He's one of the people investigating what happened yesterday."

There were so many things she wanted to say to her sister. So many questions that she might never have time to ask. *I will not cry now* she promised herself. "I love you," she told Laura. It was the most important thing she could say.

Laura's breathing was rough and uneven. Her hand let go of Jessie's and reached for her face. The effort failed before she made contact. "Jessie?" The word rasped out of her sister like a rusty gate swinging open. "You're beautiful." The effort of three words seemed to use all her strength. Jessie didn't push for more. Instead she grasped Laura's hand again gently and patted it as softly as possible.

Laura's breathing became ragged and panic played across her ruined face. "We're going to have to put you back on oxygen," the nurse said as she stepped in. "I'm sorry you didn't get to speak to her." Jessie realized that the nurse was looking over her shoulder at the deputy.

"Next time," he said.

Jessie felt like thanking him for his brave words. There probably wouldn't be a next time, but there was no sense in saying that in front of Laura. In a few minutes her sister was breathing easier again, pure air going to her lungs and pain-killing drugs coursing through her system. Jessie sat in the hard plastic chair still patting Laura's hand and willing herself not to cry. She felt so many regrets, and most of them went back more years than she wanted to admit.

Unbidden, her mind swirled back to an incident twenty years before. She could almost hear the leaves crunching under their feet as they walked home from school to the foster home where they shared a set of bunk beds.

Even then she'd been hard on her sister. "So you had that dream again. It's just a dream, Laura. Nobody will *ever* believe it's real. I'm not sure I even believe it's real anymore." Their foster mother, Mrs. Dinkins, always said that Jessie was the smart one and Laura was the pretty one. Being smart didn't seem to matter even back then, because Laura could charm her way out of almost anything.

That day Jessie got gum in her hair and Laura had somehow known what to do. She always *knew* stuff like that, the things you couldn't learn from books.

While Jessie haunted the library, Laura's favorite reading was Mrs. Dinkins's glossy magazines. If they went to the drugstore Laura always went to the magazine counter to read the ones with models or movie stars on the front.

Usually Laura's knowledge served her better than Jessie's book learning. That day she'd gotten the gum out of Jessie's hair in a flash, working in egg white like shampoo while their foster mother was upstairs soothing a fussy toddler.

Jessie could still picture her sister in the kitchen that afternoon squirting green dish soap in the sink, bubbles rising around her hands. That was Laura's favorite thing, getting everything all clean and in a row.

If her sister had problems, she hadn't thought to ask about them. Then, as now, Jessie just dumped her own problems on her sister instead. The memory of the incident probably lasted longer than the reality that afternoon. Jessie looked down at the figure on the bed, not seeing her through the blur of tears. "Those really good times never lasted long," she whispered. And now she knew those times were over for good.

THREE

At ten that morning the deputy insisted on taking Jessie home. "I don't care if you come back in an hour, but you need to get a shower, some different clothes and have your own car here." His expression said he didn't want any arguments and Jessie couldn't think of any good ones anyway. She couldn't remember being this tired and worn-out before.

"Will you go back to the hospital?" she asked on the ride back to the condo. It seemed longer going home, but then they paid attention to speed limits and traffic laws this time.

"Not right away," Steve said. He sounded as tired as she felt. "I have about six cases I'm actively working right now and several need my attention. Plus I need to talk to the fire investigators and verify that this was arson. And we need to make sure there wasn't anyone else hurt or killed in the fire. Most of the apartments in the complex were empty, it being the middle of the day, but there are always exceptions."

Jessie shivered, thinking that some other family might be going through this the way she and Laura were. Her thoughts took her to a dark place and the deputy had to put a hand on her shoulder to let her know they had stopped in her driveway. It took a moment to come back to full alertness. It took even longer to make sure she had her key and thank the man for all he had done so far.

"I'd say I do this for all my cases, but that isn't quite true," he said. He was close enough to her, standing on her front porch, that she could see things about Stephen Gardner that she hadn't noticed before. His dark eyes had little green flecks in them, and he had tiny, thin lines that could have been smile lines starting to crinkle just a bit at the corners of his warm eyes.

Right now he didn't look as if he'd smiled in quite some time. "If you don't give most people this kind of attention, why are you doing it now?" Jessie didn't know why she asked the question, but suddenly the answer was important.

"Something about your sister…and you…has me deeply involved. So involved that I should probably turn the case over to somebody else, but I can't." He straightened his shoulders and looked back toward the car. "Right now I need to go work on this, and the other cases I'm investigating. I'll see you soon."

Jessie nodded. She didn't know what to say. Stephen stood on her doorstep long enough to watch her put the key in the lock, open the door and verify that everything was all right. Then he left and she came into the condo past the front hall and sat on the sofa.

Jessie figured she would spend about half an hour at home and head back to the hospital. The rooms echoed with loneliness without Laura around. Would she ever come back here?

Looking over to the living room bookcase Jessie saw the photo album between two college textbooks on the bottom shelf. Getting up, she pulled it out and opened it to the first page and got a shock. The picture of the two of them on their picnic was right there in the album. But how could that be? Surely Laura would have told her if she had a copy made. This didn't make sense. The print didn't look as if it had been removed from the album and replaced any time recently, either.

She felt so tired she didn't know whether she could trust her own senses. Maybe there really was a logical explanation for this. Jessie just couldn't think of one now. Instead she went into her bedroom and pulled out clean clothes. After a hot shower she pushed away the temptation to crawl into the beckoning bed and went to the kitchen instead. She packed a bag full of the kind of snacks she usually took to school when she had long office hours and added a couple of peanut butter sandwiches. Now that she knew the gravity of her sister's condition, she planned her stay at the hospital to be a longer one.

Hunting for the car charger to her cell phone, she remembered she'd given it to Laura last week. No sense in trying to find that. She made a mental note to ask Deputy Gardner about Laura's car. Somewhere in an apartment complex parking lot there was a sporty blue compact unless it had been destroyed by the fire, as well.

Jessie checked the contents of her bag and picked up her address book. By tonight she would need to call the department chair and a few others so that she could arrange for somebody to cover her classes for a while. She drove back to the hospital on automatic pilot, thankful that no traffic cop caught sight of her on the way.

"Dr. Anderson? I don't recognize you. Can I help you with something?" The sharp-eyed nurse's comment almost made Cassidy drop the medical chart. Why did the woman have to show up now, in this small window of time?

"I'm doing a neuro consult for Dr. Peterson on another case and this woman caught my eye," Cassidy said with conviction. A firm voice could get one through almost any situation.

The nurse's eyes narrowed. "Surely you don't think anybody's going to ask you to do a neurological exam on my patient?"

"Not a full exam, no. But I'm working on a paper on the neuropathology of specific trauma survivors and wondered if your patient might fit as part of my study. Once I looked at her chart more closely, I could see that won't be the case." Cassidy handed the chart back to the nurse. "I won't disturb her."

The nurse's silent glare said that no one would be disturbing her patient while she was around. Cassidy walked away quickly, the way any busy specialist in a large hospital would. No one followed. Into the stairwell and down a flight quickly, Cassidy made it onto the staff parking lot before anyone could notice. The close call had been worth it; one look showed that the patient wasn't going to cause any problems for anyone.

Laura didn't show any more signs of being alert. "She's not in terrible pain," the nurse assured Jessie.

"With third-degree burns the nerve endings are numbed enough that things aren't as painful. We're almost glad to hear that someone's in a fair amount of pain because it usually means they've got more second-degree burns than third. Pain is easier to treat than the more severe burns."

So what sounded like good news at first didn't look like good news at all. Jessie asked about getting her sister off the breathing tube again, but that request was turned down. "She sounds like she could be developing pneumonia. We can't risk it" was the doctor's terse reply. After that he whisked Jessie out of Laura's cubicle for a while for treatment. She went back to the family waiting room, which seemed quiet for a change.

"Ms. Barker? Jessie?" She knew she needed rest when she startled awake stiffly from her position on the couchlike vinyl bench attached to the wall. Even sitting straight up with the television high on the wall droning through news headlines, she'd fallen asleep. And judging from the urgent tone in the nurse's voice it must have been for a while. "You need to come back with us now."

Somewhere during Jessie's last vigil at her sister's bedside, it got dark outside. Laura didn't ever look her way again with any kind of understanding in her eyes or say anything even when they switched the oxygen tube for one that would have let her talk. When they asked Jessie if there was anyone they should call, at first she shook her head. Then she called the nurse back and gave her Deputy Gardner's business card.

He was there in a very short time. He looked as if he'd dressed hurriedly when he was called, no tie and a shirt that hadn't been pressed. "You came," Jessie said. "Thank you. I didn't want to be alone right now."

"You aren't alone. You won't be alone," he said simply.

"Do you want to sit down?" It seemed odd to be talking about such mundane things while her sister lay dying.

"No, I'll stand." He looked at the figure on the bed. "It always seems more respectful somehow." The way he said it made Jessie wonder how many people Steve Gardner had seen die. Personally she hoped she would never have to do this again. She felt ripped apart by grief as she watched Laura.

"Do you want me to call someone else? One of the chaplains or somebody from my church?"

Jessie shook her head, watching her sister's struggle to breathe. "I don't want anybody else, especially not some stranger."

"All right." It was the last thing he said out loud for quite a while. So when the end came, Jessie wasn't alone there by the bedside. The deputy didn't say anything but his presence seemed to lend a strength Jessie needed. She didn't even comment when he stood there with a firm but gentle hand on her shoulder, obviously in prayer. In Jessie's eyes Laura was far beyond most human help, and if he thought prayer might do something he was welcome to it. Nothing could hurt Laura now anyway.

After it was all over, hospital personnel led Jessie into the family waiting room where she sat again on one of the couches feeling numb and brittle as an ice carving. After a few minutes one of the nurses asked if she wanted to have a moment with Laura now that they'd taken out all the tubes and needles. Jessie almost said no, but something made her change her mind. Maybe it would hurt less some time down the line if she had a different last memory of Laura than the one she had now.

Jessie passed the deputy, writing something on a piece of paper at the nurses' station. She hadn't thought about all the paperwork that must have to get done at a time like this. It pained her that her sister's life was reduced to paperwork for a sheriff's deputy. Saying nothing, she went in to see Laura. The form on the bed looked as peaceful as possible.

It was good to think that she was done with the horrible suffering of the last three days. Jessie reached out to touch a cool leg where the sheet had slipped. Her sister's unburned flesh looked like pale marble in contrast to the bandages higher up on her body.

In that act of reaching out, her fingers froze and her brain refused to process what she was seeing. Perhaps she was even more confused than she thought. She went to the other side of the bed and looked down at the still body. Anger and bewilderment welled up in her. "Deputy Gardner?" When he didn't answer, she said it louder.

He came into the cubicle still holding his papers. "What is it?"

"This isn't Laura. I don't know who this was, but it isn't my sister."

His brow wrinkled and he looked as if he wanted to say all kinds of things. Instead he stood there silently for a moment before he asked a simple question. "Why do you say that?"

Jessie lifted her right pant leg, exposing her ankle and the tiny bluebird tattooed there. "Look at this. We got them on vacation two summers ago. It was one of those stupid things you regret afterward when it's already done." Laura hadn't regretted hers, though. In fact she'd shown it off.

He looked at the body on the bed before saying anything more, and then, understanding growing, looked back at Jessie. "Your sister had one, too?"

"On her ankle, just like I did." Jessie pointed to the ankle of the person on the bed. The pale skin was unmarked by fire or anything else. Who just died in this hospital room? And where was her sister, Laura?

Steve Gardner's brain hurt. An hour after the death of the person he'd thought was Laura Barker he'd made the first round of phone calls to get crime scene investigators involved. Although the hospital itself wasn't the scene of a crime, the fact that this death was an obvious homicide meant all the sheriff's department's resources needed to be called into play.

It had been difficult to explain to the medical examiner's staff why he needed as much care taken as he did. Nothing about this case so far made any sense. At first things seemed merely confusing; a young man who appeared to have come from nowhere was missing and a woman who'd only known him a couple of days was left in his apartment near death.

The fire someone had set to destroy evidence hadn't left many clues except the identity of the woman and now that was in question. Not just in question according to Jessie. She was firm in saying that the body didn't belong to her sister. In some cases he'd question a distraught relative's statement, thinking that they just wanted to believe against hope that the person they cared about couldn't possibly be dead. But Jessie wasn't hysterical or in denial. Instead she seemed perfectly calm.

He realized that Jessie was staring at him, waiting for him to make some kind of decision about what to do next. Here he was, with his first case like this as a lead investigator, and it was threatening to implode on him. If Jessie Barker was right, then he'd have to involve the Major Case Squad. Only the combined efforts of the best homicide experts in the five counties that made up the St. Louis area would feel qualified to deal with this. Steve groaned inwardly. The last thing he wanted to do was make an immediate call to the county sheriff, but he didn't have any other choice. "How sure are you that this isn't your sister?" he asked Jessie, knowing even then what her answer would be.

"I'm positive." Her gray-blue eyes were rimmed with red and her brown hair was in disarray, but Jessie spoke with a certainty Steve wasn't ready to question. She had radiated authority the whole time he'd known her and it had impressed him. Most of the relatives he saw in tough cases went to pieces, but not this woman.

No one else was around who could dispute her claim anyway. To do that, he'd have to talk with Laura's coworkers at the day spa and see if there were any friends there that knew her well enough to verify that she'd had that tattoo. Even then, he'd have more of a mess on his hands. If this wasn't Laura Barker who was it? And what happened to the real Laura, and Adrian Bando?

So far Bando hadn't turned up alive *or* dead, and trying to trace him hadn't been promising, either. It was as if he'd just shown up out of the blue less than six months ago without any history before that. No driver's license in any state, no Social Security number in the name he went by now and no other records that matched his name or fingerprints left in the apartment. Whoever Bando had been before that, he had a clean record and hadn't been in the military.

Steve shook his head, trying to clear the fog. "You know, one thing is pretty certain. If that isn't your sister…"

"It isn't. I know for sure now that it isn't," Jessie said firmly.

"I wasn't arguing with you, Ms. Barker. I was just thinking out loud. And if you'll let me finish…" Steve felt bad immediately about the tone he'd used. No one who'd just gone through what Jessie Barker had needed more grief.

He stayed silent a moment trying to compose himself, asking God to settle his troubled feelings so that he could do his job with the skill it demanded. "As I said, if that isn't your sister there's not much either of us can do here to figure out who it is, and where Laura might be now. I need to go back to work, and you should probably go home and get some rest."

Tears filled Jessie's eyes and Steve felt even worse than before. He had no way to comfort this woman on what was probably the worst day of her life. "I know you're right, but I feel so confused. Whoever this is, she must have looked a lot like Laura before all this happened to her." Her eyes widened and she sat down quickly.

"What is it?"

"I know it's not Laura, but I just realized something. The one time she spoke to me, she called me by name." Steve leaned in close as the tears started to slide down her cheeks. He just caught her last whispered words. "She said I was beautiful."

He felt an almost overpowering urge to gather this near stranger into his arms and give her someone to lean on. "Is there anybody at all we can call to be with you?"

Jessie shook her head. She looked at him with an intensity that made him wary. There was something that she wasn't telling him. But then she sighed and her mood shifted. "There's no one. I told you before that we lost our parents when we were children. We spent most of our childhood in the foster care system until Laura turned eighteen and we've lived together ever since."

"No boyfriend?" Why did he care about the answer suddenly?

"Nobody serious for either of us. I'm too busy and Laura, believe it or not, was a little shy around men." Her expression brightened a little. "No, I guess I can still say Laura *is* a little shy."

"That's true," Steve agreed, even though his practical cop's nature felt like telling her that just because the figure on the bed wasn't her sister didn't mean Laura was alive. He prayed silently that when they opened the trunk of the car they'd impounded after the fire there wouldn't be anybody in it.

Jessie hadn't heard the change in his tone and he felt thankful about that. "Do you think you'll be okay to drive home?"

She didn't answer him right away. "Probably," she said after a while. "I'm still trying to take in the fact that my sister is out there somewhere. After the last couple days, I've been getting myself used to thinking of her…not here." She wasn't the first person he'd seen who refused to say the word *dead* to talk about a loved one.

"How do you figure out who this person really is?" she asked, forcing him to pay attention to the process, as well.

"First we'll call evidence techs from the county coroner's office in to process her. We'll take fingerprints and compare them to those on file in different databases. We'll take blood and tissue samples to do DNA tests. And just to be sure we'll need to take blood from you, as well, just to make the fact that this isn't your sister official."

Jessie nodded. He felt thankful that she wasn't arguing with what he told her. "How long will the results of those tests take?"

"Days. Unlike the TV crime shows where they get their results in fifty-five minutes, real life works a little slower. I imagine you wish it didn't."

A half smile lifted one corner of her mouth slightly. "You're right. The sooner we know who this is, or can at least prove it isn't Laura, the sooner you might be able to find her." The specter of whether the police might find Laura alive or not hung in the air between them as an unspoken threat. Steve decided not to pursue that for now.

The evidence technicians came into the room and Steve eased Jessie out so that the techs could do their work. Even now that they knew the figure on the bed was a stranger, he didn't want Jessie to have to witness the things that would happen next.

"Is there anything else you want to tell me about your sister, or your own life?" The words were out of his mouth before Steve was quite sure why he'd asked them. Didn't he already have enough to do? Still, his experience as an investigator made him value those hunches that drove him to ask a last question.

Jessie shrugged. "Not really." Her expression said something else. There was information she kept to herself right now, but he didn't know Jessie well enough to know how important her private information might be. Given her cryptic look it could be anything from a stash of unpaid traffic tickets to her sister being involved in criminal activity. What he'd seen of Jessie so far led him to believe that her secret might be closer to the traffic tickets, or something even more trivial. At least he hoped so; Jessie Barker intrigued him and for a change he wanted that feeling to come from something positive, not somebody's criminal nature. Still, watching Jessie walk away gave Steve an uncanny feeling that something very serious was wrong.

FOUR

Jessie knew she should go back to work, but she couldn't quite push herself to do it yet. Laura wasn't dead, but she was still missing and no one seemed to have any idea where she might be. The condo felt so empty without her sister there. It took only two days for Jessie to realize how much Laura usually did around the place.

When the flowers on the kitchen countertop wilted Jessie threw them out, and had no idea where to get more. When she reached for one of her favorite coffee cups on the third day and couldn't find it, it took another hour to figure out that the cups were clean in the dishwasher. Laura always unloaded it. How many of the little pleasures of her life were due to her sister? Almost all of them, apparently. Without Laura life was amazingly mundane. There was no loud music in the house when she came home from errands, the shutters stayed closed even when it was sunny. In three days the quiet got to her so much she began to think about going to the pound and adopting a dog. She had even decided what kind of dog; something large and very furry of vastly mixed breed that would answer to the name of Spike or Tiger.

She was online looking up the address of the nearest animal shelter when the phone rang. When the caller ID showed that it was the country sheriff's department she picked it up immediately. "Deputy Gardner?"

"Yes. Ms. Barker? I have something to discuss with you. Would it be all right if I came over?"

Jessie turned away from the computer, her heart beating faster. Had they found Laura? "Certainly. Do you want to set up a time to meet?"

There was silence for a few seconds. "Actually, I'd like to come over now if you don't mind."

"All right." They hung up and Jessie shut down her computer and went to the kitchen to make a pot of tea. Coffee was out of the question because she knew there was no milk in the house to offer the deputy. She sighed. "Maybe once I get the dog we can walk to the store together," she said to the empty kitchen.

Deputy Gardner refused her offer of tea, and sat in the living room in the most upright chair available. "Have you gotten a lead on Laura? Do you know where she is?"

His brow wrinkled. "Not exactly." He leaned forward in his chair. "Is there anything about your family situation that you haven't told me? Anything that might change the way our investigation is going?"

Jessie's palms began to sweat. She had only known this man for a week. There was no way she could trust him. "No. What does this have to do with finding my sister?"

"I'm not sure yet. But it has a great deal to do with identifying the victim in the morgue who isn't your sister." His eyes narrowed, making him look much more like an investigator than the compassionate man she had started getting to know in the hospital. "How much do you know about DNA?"

"Enough. I teach history, not science. But I'm sure you're going to enlighten me," Jessie snapped.

"I won't go into deep detail. But we had a surprise with that sample we took from you to prove that the victim wasn't your sister. It proved that all right, but it gave us another interesting fact. The victim shares half your DNA profile."

"Only half?" She wanted to ask more, but it was all she could choke out. Jessie always thought fainting from shock was one of those things that only happened to Victorian women who wore whalebone corsets. Surely it wasn't possible today. But suddenly she had this funny buzzing in her head and there didn't seem to be enough air in the room.

"Only half," Steve Gardner said. "Which makes the story you told me about losing your parents in a car crash just that—a story. Now I'll repeat my earlier question. Is there anything you'd like to tell me?"

The buzzing was getting louder. "Only that I'm glad there's no statute of limitations on murder because now I'm sure that someone killed my father." After that her vision blurred and Jessie quickly lay down on the couch before she pitched forward into the coffee table. The last thing she remembered thinking was that when they found Laura she didn't want to have to tell her that she'd ruined the veneer on the furniture, so she better pass out in a different direction.

Steve Gardner lunged for Jessie as she slumped sideways on her own living room couch. Before now he'd never seen anybody truly faint from stress or shock, but there was always a first for everything. Of course he'd never before confronted anybody with the news that a dead person thought to be a complete stranger was actually their parent, either.

Had that really come as a shock to the woman, or was she only buying time?

The pallor of her skin and her general wooziness as he tried to make her sit up seemed to attest to the shock being real. He looked behind him and picked up the mug of tea she'd poured herself after he'd declined her offer to pour him some, as well. It was still quite warm, but not too hot to drink. "Why don't you take this and sip it slowly. Then when you're a little more composed we can start talking about this."

She did as she was told; something he felt was probably out of character for Jessie Barker. What he'd seen so far told him that she liked to be in control of most situations. She didn't seem to be in control of this one. Her hands shook slightly as she drank a little of the aromatic tea. "Are you going to be all right?" He didn't want to go back to his seat until he was sure she wasn't going to faint again.

She took one hand and pushed back waves of deep chestnut hair away from her face. In the hospital she'd worn her hair caught back rather severely in clips. Today it was gathered loosely at the nape of her neck, and shorter strands had worked their way out to brush around her cheeks. "I think I'll be okay." She put the cup down, placing it carefully on a coaster. "I don't even know where to start to try and explain this."

"Well, that makes two of us. Why did you tell me before that your parents were dead, when you must have known that your mother was still alive?"

She gave a short, mirthless laugh. "Well, see, that's the problem. Nobody knew that but me and Laura. At least nobody else ever believed it. That car crash when we were small really happened. I'm sure you can find reports of it in the newspapers in the little town where my father taught at the state university. And in the cemetery at the edge of that same town there's a very lovely monument with both of my parents' names on it."

Okay, this made even less sense than he'd expected. "How did that happen? Were you adopted?"

"No. I wondered that, too, when I got old enough to try and figure all of this out myself, but I checked the birth certificates for my sister and me and they both list our parents. I know that can be faked but nobody ever suggested that was the case. I figured that if we'd actually had another mother somewhere, the courts would probably have notified her and she would have come and gotten us. We wouldn't have had to spend so much time in foster care." Her gray eyes flashed with anger. "I mean, nobody would have abandoned two kids like that if they didn't have to. I think our mother actually saved our lives by leaving us that night."

He must have looked even more confused, because she took a deep breath and sat back on the couch. "I'm going to tell you this story once, and afterward you can ask any question you want as long as you give me the benefit of the doubt believing me. All right?"

He didn't know why he should agree, but he had nothing to lose. If she shut down now he had no other real avenue to explore. "All right. Do you want me to keep from interrupting while you tell the story?"

"It would probably help. I haven't told anyone all of this in more than twenty years. And I've never told it to anybody who believed me."

The thought roused Steve's interest like nothing else could. What could be so fantastic that an eye-witness account wouldn't be believed, even that of a child? He got ready to write down what Jessie said, wondering where this tale would take him.

"Remember, I was only six," she began. "My parents were arguing in the front seat of the car, which wasn't unusual. It was more like squabbling most of the time, but they didn't always get along. I don't know how far away from home we were, and I don't really remember where we'd been that day. Laura and I fell asleep in the backseat and I remember waking up after hearing a bang."

"Was the car still moving?" Steve knew he shouldn't interrupt but he couldn't help himself.

Jessie didn't seem to mind the simple question. "No. We were pulled over on the side of the road, not exactly like we'd been in an accident or anything. There were several strange men there, at least three of them. One of them pulled Laura and me out of the car and we stood in some weeds and watched our life fall apart."

"Did any of them talk to you? And what about your parents?"

Jessie's brow wrinkled. "From an adult perspective I know now that my father was already dead. I think he'd been shot, but I can't tell you why I believe that. I didn't see a shot fired."

"You said you heard a bang as you woke up. Could it have been a gunshot?"

"Maybe. It's hard to know."

"How about the men. Do you remember anything about them, what they looked like or if anybody mentioned any names?"

She looked at him and her eyes filled with tears. "I'm sorry. I'll have to think about that awhile."

"I'll stop barking at you so much." He hadn't meant to push her this hard.

"No, it's not that. Nobody's ever taken me this seriously before. I don't know how to react."

He felt more pain for her now than he did when he thought he'd intimidated her. What must it be like to carry this kind of secret for over twenty years? "Take your time. Try to recall as much of the scene as you can. Close your eyes if it helps."

Jessie leaned back against the couch cushions. "I don't remember any names. They were just big and scary looking." She stopped for a moment. "Okay, there is one thing. When I just said the men were scary, something dawned on me. My mother wasn't scared. Not the way I would expect somebody to be."

"Do you think she knew them?" It would explain her not being afraid, but it led to a dozen more questions.

"I'm not sure if she knew them personally, but they were familiar to her, if that makes any sense. And now that I think of it, she definitely knew the man who was in charge. She didn't talk to him the way you'd talk to a stranger. She felt free to argue with him some."

"Argue how?" Steve had started listening to this story figuring it might be the fantasy of a child. But so far most of what Jessie had told him sounded plausible. He could almost see the serious girl she'd been at six, stuck in this terrible situation.

"I think he wanted to hurt us, maybe even kill us and put us back in the car with my father and the woman. I didn't tell you about her, did I?"

Steve shook his head, not wanting to interrupt at this point if he didn't have to.

"Two of the other men took a woman from one of the other cars and put her in the front seat where my mother usually sat. Again, once I grew up I knew that she was probably dead or at least incapacitated somehow. Then I didn't understand why she let them put her in the car."

"Why didn't anybody realize that the body in the car wasn't your mother?"

"It would have been hard to tell. At the time I remembered the men pushing our car down a hill. There was another loud noise and the car caught fire. Later when I found the newspaper articles they reported that the car had gone down a dangerous embankment and burned."

"How did anybody explain that you and your sister survived?"

"I'm not sure. Nobody ever wanted to talk about the accident afterward. A few weeks later the social workers were telling us to forget what happened. Child counseling must have been so different then."

"No kidding." There were a few things that just didn't sound right about Jessie's story, but Steve didn't want to tell her that now. Especially when she trusted him enough to tell him what she'd hidden for so long. "So what happened after that?"

Jessie sighed. "I don't remember seeing any cars pass once the men put my mother in a car and they all drove away. Somebody must have seen or heard something, though, because after a while there were fire trucks and police cars there and they put us in the back of a police cruiser and took us to some kind of juvenile hall once they figured out we weren't hurt."

"Physically, at least. What you saw had to be an incredible shock."

"It was. Laura didn't say anything for about four days. And she was usually the chatterbox of the family. For a while I was afraid she wasn't ever going to talk again. I stopped wanting to say anything more myself after the third or fourth time I told my story and an adult told me that it wasn't true."

Steve couldn't keep from wincing. It had always been part of his nature to be as honest as possible, even with kids. What had motivated these people to deny Jessie's story? "Were there services for your parents anywhere? Did anybody try to comfort you or take care of you?"

Jessie lifted one shoulder in a shrug. "I don't think there were any services. We weren't ever religious, and there wasn't any other close family. If there was anything at the college where my father taught, they didn't take us there. Like I said before, they were already telling us to forget that it happened, as if that would ease the pain. We went into foster care, and fortunately we always stayed together. I think Laura could have been adopted if it wasn't for me. She was still young and cute enough to be attractive."

Steve felt anger rising in himself. "You say that like you think you weren't. But Jessie, you were only six years old."

Her smile was slow and sad. "Right, but I was an old six and I was smart as well as realistic. You saw the picture of the two of us together. Laura was tiny and blond and adorable. I already had glasses, straight brown hair and a serious disposition. Who would want that when they could have an adorable baby instead?"

It was all Steve could do not to wrap his arms around her and try to comfort the hurt little kid he could see looking out from her gaze. He wanted to stroke her hair and tell her that she was a beloved child of God, but he sensed it wasn't time yet. Some day Jessie Barker would be ready to hear those words, and after hearing her story he hoped he'd be the one to convince her of just how valuable she'd always been in God's eyes.

His throat was so tight with emotion that he had to wait a minute before he could speak. "I wish somebody had told you back then just how wonderful you were. And I'm impressed by how much you remember from that long ago. Now I ought to go back and try to figure out where that leaves us with your mother. She didn't just vanish for that long and reappear for no reason."

"You're right. But what on earth could her reason have been? It never made sense to me that she disappeared, unless the man in charge was somebody she was...involved with in some way and they wanted her to vanish. But why would she come back and then not come and find us right away?" Jessie's gray-blue eyes told him that she was as confused by that as he felt.

"I don't know. But I intend to find out," he told her. Steve really hadn't meant to get that close to promising her an answer. But the words were out of his mouth before he could stop them. With the number of times Jessie had already been disappointed by life, he didn't want to add to the string of hurts unless he had no other choice.

Guess that means I have my work cut out for me, Steve thought. He was about to say more, but one look at Jessie's eyes filled with tears made him stop. "How do you trace somebody who just disappears for so long? Is it even worth pursuing when my sister's still missing?"

Steve nodded, the beginnings of an idea stirring

his brain. "It's worth pursuing all right. In fact I think solving the mystery of your mother could lead us to Laura." There were still a lot of gaps to fill in, but at least he had somewhere to start.

What was wrong now? Watching the door of the condo was making Cassidy nervous. The deputy had been in there way too long. This was just another in the long string of catastrophes in this matter. It had been obvious that there were problems when days passed and there had been no funeral announcement for Laura Barker. Even with an autopsy and all the crime scene reports, her sister should have claimed the body and gotten on with things by now.

Cassidy was tired of watching boring people conduct their petty little lives in the insipid suburbs of a second-rate city. Cheap hotels were no substitute for the comfortable apartment Cassidy was used to. A vibrating cell phone broke the mood.

The man on the other end sounded calm. A stranger listening to his even tone of voice would think he was just fine. The edge of tension Cassidy could hear spelled big trouble. "They know. I thought you said everything was taken care of."

Cassidy nearly dropped the phone in surprise. "It was. There's no way they could know, especially this quickly."

Patrick nearly growled. "Well, you're wrong. Again. I've got copies of the report issued this morning proving the woman at the coroner's office is Dawn Barker."

Think fast and don't panic. Cassidy scrambled for an answer, knowing that anyone who upset Patrick this badly could often count their life in hours. "Find out what Jessica knows, and how much of it she's told that deputy. Call me back by this time tomorrow to tell me how you plan to make this right."

"I will," Cassidy promised, letting Patrick end the call. He wasn't the kind of man anybody hung up on, even when he was in a good mood. In a mood like this one, it could be a fatal mistake.

FIVE

Two days later Jessie felt more energized than she had in weeks. She threw herself into work, trying to take back her life as best she could. That wasn't going to be an easy task. If home seemed strange, work wasn't all that comforting, either. Even the faces weren't all the same. They'd hired a new department secretary just before she'd left and she still didn't know the woman. Then there were classes to teach, papers to grade and students to talk to. She tried not to scoff at any of their crises, which seemed so petty after what she'd gone through lately. She had to keep reminding herself that for these community college students, the problems they brought to her were major things.

After she thought about it for a while she realized that what she'd gone through could make her a better teacher and a more sympathetic mentor if she let it.

That made her want to call Steve Gardner and ask him more about the things that seemed to give him the compassion he showed her. What might he have gone through that made him that vigilant and caring at the same time? And how much of it had to do with that faith he exhibited? For the first time in her adult life someone had her wondering if maybe belief in God was something more than just superstition and a crutch for people to lean on. It didn't look that way for Steve. Before she could give the matter any more thought her cell phone rang.

When she saw who was calling the hairs on the back of her neck rose. It took another ring for her to compose herself. "Hello?" Jessie held her breath, reminding herself that the county sheriff's office had lots of employees and one of them besides Steve could be calling her.

"Hi. Jessie?" Steve's familiar voice made her remember to breathe.

"Hi, Steve. That's so uncanny. I was thinking of you when my phone rang. What's up? Have you heard anything new about Laura?"

"No, but something else has come up that I need to talk to you about. Would you have time this afternoon?"

"I can make time." Jessie looked at her planner, trying to figure out where she could juggle an hour or so. "My last class is over at three-thirty. And being a college campus, there's no shortage of coffeehouses around here. Would meeting in one of them be all right?"

"Sure." They settled on a time and place, leaving Jessie slightly distracted for the rest of her day wondering what Steve had to say. She got to the coffee shop before he did, and settled in with a mocha, splurging on whipped cream for the top. Normally she didn't go for that many calories but she hadn't been eating much lately. Eating almost every meal by herself was lonely business.

She'd only had a couple of sips when Steve walked in. She hadn't seen him for a little while and was struck by how handsome he looked, even in his deputy's uniform. She wondered if they'd ever be in a situation where he would come into a room where she was and he'd be smiling. So far he'd had little to smile about when he'd been around her, and today didn't seem to be different.

He looked around the room and saw Jessie at her corner table. Walking over he stood by the well-worn wooden chair and the briefest of smiles played around his face then vanished. "Once this is all over, we have got to meet under better circumstances at least once," he said, echoing her thoughts.

Jessie nodded. "You're right. Do you want to get

something hot before you sit down? If I'd known what you wanted I would have just ordered for you."

"I'm not picky. You could get me just about anything that has coffee in it and I'd be happy. After a few years of some of the stuff they pass off as coffee at the department, if it's black and hot I'll drink it."

Jessie shuddered, making him grin for a second. "Not me. I've even taken to bringing coffee to work so that we can have something besides what the college will supply. Their budget doesn't allow for anything special." She gave a quiet laugh. "Laura says…" and then she faltered thinking about her sister.

Steve sat down quickly. "Go on, Jessie. Tell me what Laura says. If it's in my power to do it, I'll see that she can tell me herself someday but I want to hear it now." He took her hand to encourage her and Jessie fought the urge to give in to tears.

"Okay. Laura says we're all just too silly with the coffee craze. She's a tea drinker, and her favorite is that neon-green Japanese stuff that I think tastes like burned grass."

"Matcha," Steve said solemnly. "I don't really care for it, either, but it's a nice color." He rose from the chair. "I'll get myself a plain old coffee and be back in a minute." He did just that. Jessie gave him a minute or two to get his thoughts collected and drink some of his coffee while it was still hot.

"You said you needed to talk to me, and that there was nothing new about Laura. Were you telling me the truth, or is it just something too bad to tell me over the phone?"

Steve's eyes darkened. "I won't lie to you, Jessie, ever. And I don't sugarcoat things, either. If I'd known something bad about Laura I would have called you to warn you and then come over myself to tell you the news."

Obviously, she'd touched a nerve. "Okay. For now that's reassuring. But what is it that you want to tell me?" It had to be about her mother, she reasoned. That or perhaps a lead on Adrian's whereabouts, but Jessie figured that was the least important thing Steve could tell her.

He took a deep breath and drank a little more of his coffee. "Well, you see it's like this. Finding out that Laura wasn't the one who died in the hospital was a good thing. And finding out that it was your mother who actually died was a good thing in most ways. But it brings up a really rotten part of department policy that I can't get around."

"What is that?" Jessie racked her brain, trying to come up with something that might make the deputy this uncomfortable.

He looked down at the table. "Once a person is identified, they are no longer the final responsibility of the county. If a family member is located, that person becomes the responsible party."

Jessie sat back in her chair, realizing why Steve looked downcast. "Meaning that when you're done with my mother's body, I'll have to deal with it, right?"

Steve nodded. "You're right. When I found out that the department was going to notify you of that through the regular channels via the medical examiner, I told the head of the detective bureau that I'd do it myself. I feel like I have a stake in this case and it seemed right." He smiled in a way that made him look more woeful than happy. "It's my first official act as a detective. The paperwork went through finally and I got the full promotion. Starting next week I'll be plainclothes."

"I'm glad you got your promotion," Jessie said, meaning every word she said. "I'm only sorry that you had to come over here and tell me this as your first assignment as a detective. I appreciate you coming in person to do it, though. This whole experience has been so surreal."

She took a sip of her cooling mocha. "It seems really unfair. I never got to know my mother as an adult, and now I have to say goodbye to her before I ever had a chance to say hello."

"It does seem wrong somehow. Especially when we have no idea where she came from before she ended up here in St. Charles. It would help to know if she had insurance somewhere, or family you didn't know about. She could have an entire life under a different name and we have no way of knowing."

"I take it that means that you've used all the fancy tools at your disposal to check her out and prove she had no criminal record, no ties anywhere and her fingerprints didn't show up under some other name in any of your databases."

He gave her an assessing look. "You know all the tricks, don't you? What did you say your teaching specialty was again?"

"Popular culture, especially urban legends. I'm one of those people that don't believe anything until somebody can prove it to me. To be able to disprove stories, you have to know how to check them out."

"Wow. I'll have to remember to keep you in my file even when this case is finished. I could use a source that knowledgeable in a lot of my work." Steve smiled, and this time it looked real. "Of course, I would like to keep you in my file for a lot of reasons. Department regulations are very strict about involvement with anyone who's part of an open case. I want to wrap up all the loose ends on this one as soon as possible."

Jessie was about to tell him how kind that was, but then she realized that Detective Gardner wasn't just being kind to her in his wish to wrap this all up. He was hinting that he wanted to go out with her after he closed the case. Suddenly her face felt warmer than the cup in her hand. She was being flirted with, and if the truth be told, it was a flattering feeling.

After a brief moment, though, reality drew her back down to business. No matter how flattering it was to have Steve show a personal interest in her, they had plenty of problems to deal with before they could do anything about that. "I've never had to plan a funeral or a memorial service before. Until last week I would have said Laura was my only family in the world, so I've never given any thought to something like this."

"Would you like some help? I could put you in touch with somebody from my church, or if you'd rather have someone else, you could talk to the hospital chaplain and see what he or she recommends."

Jessie considered her options. Even though she didn't have much in the way of religious leanings herself, she had no idea what her mother might have wanted. She tried to remember anything she might have said when they were children, but absolutely nothing came to mind. They had celebrated holidays in traditional, secular ways: Santa Claus at Christmas, the Easter bunny bringing eggs, and perhaps a quick moment at Thanksgiving dinner to say what they were thankful for, nothing more.

"Do you think you could help me yourself? This all seems to come much more naturally to you, and I have no idea what my mother would have wanted." Jessie didn't usually say something that impulsively, but with Steve she'd been a different person from the first moment. "It's not like there will be anybody else at whatever I plan anyway."

"Unless someone out there is looking for your mother the way we're looking for Laura," he said, taking her aback. "It's not terribly likely, but we have to consider that. And yes, I can help you plan some kind of memorial for your mother. I still think we ought to have a little help from someone. Is it all right if I call a friend at the hospital to help with the planning?"

Jessie nodded, the whole conversation with its emotional roller-coaster ride was beginning to leave her drained. "Sure. As I said, I've never done anything like this before. For once I'll take all the help I can get."

When Steve introduced Jessie to Rachel two days later, he didn't realize his mistake until it was too late. Jessie was abrupt and chilly the moment she laid eyes on Rachel and he couldn't figure out why until he looked at her from Jessie's viewpoint. When he looked at Rachel he just saw a friend from Bible study at church who cared about people and loved the Lord. Jessie didn't know any of that, and more than likely saw her as a pretty redhead with a warm smile and an easy familiarity with Steve.

Someday, Steve told himself, *you're going to have to learn how women think.* His mother would probably tell him that if that hadn't happened for him yet at the ripe old age of thirty-four, it wasn't going to happen. But then she continually held out hope that one day he'd show up on her front porch with a woman in tow, so maybe she hadn't totally given up on him yet. Where did a guy learn how to think like one of these fascinating but confusing creatures? Certainly not at the police academy.

His musings stopped as he listened to the conversation between Jessie and Rachel, which was primarily one-sided. "Steve knows that I do a lot of service planning at my job and I appreciate him thinking of me to help you with this. He hasn't told me much about the situation, only that it was a bit unusual."

"That's putting it mildly." Jessie still looked suspicious, her arms crossed over her chest. "What is it you said you do again?"

"I work for Mercy Hospital as a family liaison and grief support specialist."

"You're a social worker," Jessie said bluntly, looking back and forth between Steve and Rachel.

"Not exactly," Rachel said slowly. "And his asking me to help out doesn't mean I'm acting for the hospital. I'm just doing this as a friend." She reached over and gave Steve a quick pat on the arm, and he could see Jessie watch the motion and tense up even more.

"I see." Her voice sounded chilly. Steve knew he needed to do something, but he wasn't sure what to say to put things back on the right track. He breathed a quick, fervent prayer asking for guidance and help in this situation, knowing that his own skills were woefully inadequate at the present.

Rachel's warm laugh flooded him with a feeling of calm. "You sound suspicious, but it's not like that at all. I owe this guy a lot. He introduced me to the man I'm going to marry, and he even slowed the guy down long enough for me to catch him."

"Oh, now you're going to start telling stories on me," he complained. "Don't listen to everything she says, Jessie. I'm not that aggressive on the softball field, and Pastor Tom is the only guy I've ever put on the disabled list, honest."

Jessie's eyes widened and Rachel's laugh grew

even warmer. "He ran into a player on the opposing team who was trying to steal home. I don't think he meant to knock the wind out of Tom as hard as he did, but I'm giving Steve the benefit of the doubt. Tom's ankle puffed up almost immediately and since I was already warming the bench and worked at the closest hospital, I got elected to take him to the emergency room. It was a busy night there, we talked a lot, and the rest, as they say, was history."

"Yeah, and now we're probably going to lose her at our church when she marries Tom because he's still the youth pastor at a big church across town."

"What we do for love," Rachel said with a sigh. "But I'm being way too cheerful when I'm supposed to be here to help you work out something serious." She motioned to the hall that Steve knew led back away from this common area to Jessie's private office in the history department. "Do you want to go somewhere that we can sit and talk quietly?"

Jessie's whole posture had changed. She still looked solemn and somewhat worn, but the tight, defensive stance was gone. "I'd like that. Is it okay if Steve comes back with us? That is, if he has time."

"I've got time. And I wouldn't have it any other way," Steve assured her, following the women down the short hall past the empty secretary's desk into

Jessie's office. He sent up another silent prayer, this time in thanks.

As they walked, a verse from Ephesians from the last Bible study he'd done with Rachel and others from their singles class at church a few weeks before echoed in his mind:

Now all glory to God, Who is able, through His mighty power at work within us, to accomplish infinitely more than we might ask or think.

Amen to that, he thought. This awkward start to a situation turned out far better than he ever could have accomplished alone.

After about twenty minutes of discussion to fill Rachel in on more of the situation, they started talking about what kind of memorial might be appropriate for Jessie's mother. "I wish we could just wait until Laura was back home, safe and sound but we still can't count on that," Jessie said quietly.

"This would be a lot easier if you had your sister's help, wouldn't it? I know I can't be any kind of substitute for her help, but I can at least point you toward some resources." Again Steve gave thanks for Rachel and her calm demeanor. She was just the right person to support Jessie now that they'd gotten the personal tensions out of the way. Rachel had real gifts for helping people and they came through in almost everything she did.

"You're right." Jessie pushed a folder of papers around on her desk. "This would be a lot easier if I had Laura's help. At least I wouldn't have to do everything, and there would be somebody who could really understand what I'm going through."

"There's already somebody who understands, Jessie, but you might not want to hear about it now. If you want to learn about what Jesus went through just for you, and how He stands by you no matter what's going on, promise you'll ask me, or Steve." He sat there amazed that Rachel had found the perfect opportunity to do what he'd been too reluctant to do so far.

Even more surprising was Jessie's reaction. "I'll do that. I'm not ready today, but seeing what you and Steve have is making me ask a lot of questions."

"Cool. Is it okay if I pray for you, and your sister?"

Jessie smiled briefly. "Yes. I'd like that."

God's power was at work all over this situation, Steve thought. He wondered what the Lord had in store for them next.

SIX

In the end there were only four people at the grave-side six days later when they buried her mother. Steve's friend Rachel stayed with them, just the way she promised she would, and she listened as her fiancé spoke a few words there. Jessie wasn't sure what she'd expected Tom to be, but he seemed perfectly ordinary and quite pleasant, with boyish good looks and sparkling eyes. They had talked twice before the memorial service and she was impressed by his friendliness and approachability.

Jessie thought he was probably very good at working with teens and she told him so. His answering smile was a little shy and she could see why he and Rachel made a good couple. She was still mystified by their ability to believe so whole-heartedly in God when there just wasn't any proof of His existence. For as long as she could remember she had relied on those things she could prove but now there were fewer and fewer of them every day.

Steve stood beside Jessie, just close enough that she could reach out if she needed to touch him. For a while she thought she'd be all right alone, but then Tom began the quiet words of ritual and everything got to her at once. Standing there in the chill in her dark clothing she couldn't take it all in. In her ignorance she'd thought the words "ashes to ashes, dust to dust" were part of the Bible until Tom gently told her otherwise. They still seemed fitting, the right thing to be said over the remains of this mother who remained a mystery to her.

Anger and resentment welled up in her that she had to do this by herself. Even after talking to Rachel she still felt that Laura should be here to help her deal with this, to make sense of it all. Rachel had been totally right about one thing: nobody else could possibly understand it all the same way that her sister would. Jessie found herself holding tightly to Steve's hand as hot tears ran down her cheeks.

Steve reached into the pocket of his dark pants with the hand that wasn't holding Jessie's and got a white handkerchief, handing it to her. She wiped away the tears, looking at him while she thought. All three people standing here on this hill in the cool fall air claimed to believe in a loving God Who guided

them through life. How could they possibly believe
that? Where was any evidence of that loving God in
this situation? Jessie felt too confused to even ask
the question out loud as Tom finished his words and
she said goodbye to a mother she'd never really
known.

Cassidy hid behind a couple of cheap pots of ivy
and a trowel, silently bemoaning the state of modern
cemeteries. They were just too tidy, with no large
trees to use for any kind of surveillance. Watching
Jessica and her pet deputy meant going to a lot of
trouble to blend into the scenery. First there was a ne-
glected grave to pick out near Dawn's burial site, and
clothes to buy to look like a relative caring for the
grave.

The death notice in the paper had caused a great
deal of consternation for Cassidy. They'd figured out
Dawn's identity quickly, and the obituary had raised
questions. Had it been a try at drawing the murderer
out in the open, or truly the work of a grieving
daughter? The lack of a crowd at least said that the
media hadn't caught wind of the fact that a woman
who'd been missing and presumed dead for over
twenty years had surfaced, only to die for real.

This time Cassidy had taken the coward's way
out and forwarded Patrick a link to the newspaper's

obituary Web site, using the agreed upon e-mail address no one could trace to Patrick. This made for one less incendiary phone conversation, but left Cassidy in dread of the call Patrick was sure to make soon in response.

The young minister droned on. What on earth could he possibly say for this long about a total stranger? Finally he stopped rambling and closed his prayer book, or whatever it was. The young woman with him distributed hugs all around like party favors and the pair left, leaving Jessica and the deputy next to a mound of bare, disturbed earth. Jessica hadn't gone to a lot of trouble with this funeral, Cassidy thought, apparently wanting to get things over with quickly and cheaply. Why hadn't she just had the body cremated? It was even cheaper and destroyed a lot of evidence.

The light wind blew in the wrong direction for Cassidy to catch all of the conversation between the deputy and Jessica. Still, bits and pieces helped tell the story. "…back to work?" the man asked Jessica. "I'm going to insist we have something to eat first."

If he'd just leave her alone for a few days, this whole mess would be easy to fix. A depressed, distraught woman with a history of instability could hardly be faulted for taking her own life. And once

Jessica Barker was gone, the last loose end would be tied up. Even Patrick would have nothing to complain about then.

Jessie sat across the table from Steve, wondering if letting him take her to lunch was a mistake. If Rachel and Tom had been with them it might have felt more like the end of a memorial service for her mother. But they had gone back to work at the church and the hospital, and Steve insisted that she wasn't going anywhere without eating first. Maybe she did look as peaked as he claimed. She felt drained enough that it was possible.

She knew she looked awful. The dark blue outfit she wore only emphasized the paleness of her skin and the damp chill in the air flattened her hair even more than usual. Her eyes were probably pink from crying, and she just felt emotionally bruised somehow. But the place he took her for lunch changed her mood from the moment they'd walked into its warmth and coziness.

"Okay, I've worked at the community college for four years, and I end up rotating between the cafeteria and three other places nearby. How did I miss this one?"

Steve smiled. "I don't know. Maybe you got

yourself into a rut. Or maybe you judge a little more by appearances than you think you did."

"You could be right," Jessie admitted. "I've probably walked or driven past this place a few dozen times, and from the outside it doesn't look like much." The plain brick front of the building, with its standard plate glass windows appeared nondescript. Most of the neighboring businesses weren't the restaurants or antique shops that dotted this part of town, but more everyday concerns like a copy shop and a store that sold lighting.

"I have a little advantage on this one," Steve said. "Miss Ella the owner has a couple of department connections. Her late husband was a deputy and her daughter is one of our best dispatchers. So I might have been here a time or two."

"Still, I've got to thank you for expanding my horizons." The homey atmosphere inside the café made Jessie lean back in her chair and relax more than she thought she could today. The pot of hot tea sending up a little steam in front of her had almost steeped long enough to pour, and Ella had already been over once to fuss over Steve and make sure he didn't need a warm-up on coffee already.

The sixtyish-looking café owner looked as if she could be in a commercial for almost anything that came out of a good cook's kitchen, with her neat graying hair, and her flowered skirt and lavender sweater partially hidden with a cheery apron. She'd already declared that Jessie needed some looking after, making her fight back the heat of tears behind her eyelids. She saw Steve's almost imperceptible shake of the head, and a few moments later when he got up to wash his hands, she noticed that he stopped and had a brief, quiet conversation with Ella.

She was beside Jessie in a moment. "Honey, I'm so sorry. Steve just told me about your mother. I should have kept my opinions to myself," the older woman said, cheeks flushed. "I forget that not everybody wants or needs my advice."

Jessie looked down at the table for a little while to collect herself, trying to find the right thing to say. "It's all right. Really it's sort of nice to have someone say I might need a little help. My mother wasn't close to my sister and me, and I appreciate the concern." No sense in going into details with someone she'd just met. Jessie wondered if her whole personality was somehow undergoing a change. Where was the strong, independent person she'd been since she was six, taking on the world virtually alone?

"Well, you let me know if you need anything else. We're past the big lunch rush by now and I'll do anything I can while you're here." Ella patted her softly on the shoulder and was gone before Steve came back to the table.

He slid back into his seat, brow wrinkled slightly in concern. "Everything okay? I know Ella can be a little bit overwhelming at times, but she's got a good heart."

"It's fine. And I don't really find her overwhelming. As you said, she obviously cares about people. In a way it's nice to have someone care a little about me. I'm used to being pretty independent."

"Being that way is great most of the time." Steve poured a bit of cream from the pitcher on the table into his coffee. "But when you're facing something like the challenges you've got in your life right now, independence can get in the way."

"I never believed that before but now I'm beginning to find that out. I miss Laura so much. Before she disappeared I would have said I was the responsible one who took care of everything. Now that I'm alone I'm aware of just how much my sister did for the two of us." Jessie could feel unshed tears building up again. This was just so unlike her. She expected Steve to be uncomfortable, but instead he merely reached into a pocket and pulled out his now-rumpled handkerchief.

"I've given this to you twice today when I was afraid I'd need this myself. I've gotten so deeply involved in this case that I didn't know how hearing

Tom say a few words at the cemetery was going to affect me."

"Wow. That's the last thing I expected to hear from a seasoned law enforcement officer like you." She took the cotton square and used it to wipe her eyes. "I thought they taught you to stay detached from just about anything."

Steve shrugged. "They do. And normally I can stay that way. But something about sitting with you when we still thought that was Laura at the hospital got me involved in this case. Probably more involved than I should be, but it's a little late to change that now even if I wanted to."

Jessie felt her heart thump in her chest. "Does that mean you want to stay involved? And do you mean just with the case, or with me or…I don't think I know what I mean right now. Why don't we just eat lunch?" The relief she felt as Ella brought their bowls of vegetable soup and warm homemade rolls was all out of proportion to the event.

Steve bowed his head and she realized he was probably saying grace over his food. Jessie felt thankful for the silence and the distraction from her foolish remark. The silence continued for a few minutes as they ate lunch. After a while Steve looked across the table at her and smiled. "So, do you want me to try to answer that convoluted set of questions or not?"

"I think not," Jessie said, aware of the bright pink flush to her cheeks that had nothing to do with the hot soup she was eating. "Let's just enjoy lunch together first and talk later."

"If you say so." Steve reached for the bread basket between them. "I'm hungry enough to stay quiet and eat Ella's good cooking." He ate his lunch, looking over at Jessie every so often.

"I have to imagine that this is the kind of place that has two or three different kinds of pie, all home baked," she said when she'd finished her soup. She wasn't all that hungry, but talking about dessert might distract Steve from finishing the conversation.

"You're right. This time of year there's always apple, sometimes pumpkin or sweet potato, and a third kind to round things out unless there's bread pudding instead."

"Hmm. If you know the dessert schedule by heart, it sounds like somebody has a sweet tooth," she said. "I can't fault you too much because desserts are my weakness, as well."

"Good. Then I won't feel guilty getting the apple pie with a scoop of ice cream. Maybe I can talk you into sharing it with me, or getting something of your own that we can split."

Jessie gave it some thought. "How about we just

ask for an extra spoon with yours? I don't think I could manage more than a few bites at most."

"Okay. But sometime soon you're going to have to start eating a little more or I'm going to be worried about you. You're starting to look a lot thinner than when we met."

"And that's a bad thing?" she asked.

"Yes, I'd say so. I'm not all that fond of women looking like supermodels. It just doesn't look healthy. Even if I weren't extra concerned about you, I'd say that you could be cruising toward getting sick if you don't watch out for yourself." His expression was serious when Jessie had expected him to say something teasing.

She played his words back in her mind as she tried to find the right answer for him. It sounded as though Steve was trying to tell her that she meant more to him than just someone connected with a case. How did she feel about that? She wasn't quite sure yet, but his concern deserved an answer.

"I almost always stop eating much when I'm upset about something," she told him. "Usually I'm not in situations where I'd be upset for very long, so it's not a problem. I mean, most women think they could stand to lose a few pounds. But I'll watch myself more carefully this time because I don't have Laura around to worry about me."

"Yes, and I can't take over her job. I can't give you the same kind of care a sister could."

Jessie grimaced. "Good thing. You just don't seem like the sisterly type."

Finally she got a real smile out of Steve. "Thanks. Now how about we get that pie?"

Jessie nodded. *Anything*, she thought, *to stop this conversation before she made an even bigger fool of herself.*

Where was all this going? Steve tried to figure out what was happening between him and Jessie as he drove her back to her office at the community college. The tension and what he might describe as chemistry between them pulled a little tauter whenever they spent time together. He found himself wishing that he had a sister to talk this over with.

Maybe Rachel could fulfill that function if he talked to her at church on Sunday. He wasn't used to having a woman pay attention to him, and he definitely wasn't used to being this interested in a woman. It was bad enough that she was part of a case he had charge of. Should he think about turning over the case to someone else, or just keep things cool with Jessie until this was finished?

There were problems with either of those

choices; he couldn't turn over the first case he was lead investigator on without causing himself and the department some serious problems. And keeping things on the back burner with Jessie could be pretty difficult when this case could go on for months. For her sake he hoped it ended a lot sooner than that and with her sister back safely. The odds were against that as each day passed, but he wasn't ready to tell her that yet.

For now just riding together was okay with Jessie looking more relaxed than he had expected her to today. What must it be like to bury a parent you didn't really know? At least when his father died, Steve had the benefit of a long and mostly good relationship, with few regrets and little unsaid between them. He talked to his mother enough that there weren't many surprises in their relationship, either. He'd complained growing up that his family was too much like the Cleavers but as he got older he appreciated that more and more.

"Do you want me to walk in with you?" For some reason Steve asked as they pulled up in the community college parking lot.

"Normally I'd say no, but I think this time I'll let you. Thank you for taking me to lunch. I needed the company today." He opened the door to the building for her and they went in.

When they got to the lobby area for the history department offices a man stood near the secretary's desk. Both of them looked up as Steve and Jessie walked in. Something about him put Steve on alert. He wasn't familiar, but had a look—the dark, conservative suit, white shirt and short ginger hair—that said he was in law enforcement. "That's Professor Barker," the woman at the desk said, and the man turned to meet them.

"Jessica Barker? I'm Special Agent Joshua Richards with the Federal Bureau of Investigation. We need to talk."

Steve shouldered his way into the space between the stranger and Jessie. "Steve Gardner, St. Charles County Sheriff's department. If you wouldn't mind showing us some identification first…"

"Of course." The man smiled, but the effort didn't reach his steel-blue eyes. "Those rumors you've heard about lack of cooperation between local authorities and the FBI are blown all out of proportion, Deputy."

The guy's placating statement made Steve's hackles rise even more. "It's Detective, and in much of my experience they're right on track, Agent Richards."

Jessie laid a hand on his shoulder, making him stop the staring contest he and Richards had been involved in. "I'd be satisfied to see your identification, Agent Richards. If you don't mind..." She trailed off.

Richards reached into the inside pocket of his charcoal jacket and pulled out an ID wallet. Steve looked over Jessie's shoulder while she examined it. "You really are who you say you are. But I don't remember seeing your name on the list of people working out of the regional office in St. Louis."

"That's because I'm not part of their team," Richards said, taking his ID back from Jessie. He still acted a little too smooth for Steve's taste, but perhaps he just felt overly protective of Jessie after what she'd been through.

"So where are you from?" Steve wasn't sure this FBI agent would tell him anything, but it didn't hurt to try.

"Virginia. I'm part of a special OC task force and I want Ms. Barker's permission to do something she's not going to like."

"And what would that be?" Jessie's voice wasn't nearly as friendly as it had been. It sounded even more wary than it had when she first met Rachel. Steve felt like turning to her and complimenting her for good common sense, but he kept his remarks to himself. No sense in needlessly aggravating a federal officer. Given Richards's attitude so far there would probably be plenty of opportunities when they couldn't avoid aggravating him.

"I have an order here to exhume the body of Dawn Barker, in order to prove that she was the woman the task force also recognizes as Paula Brandino."

Steve watched Jessie's face. It didn't show any recognition when Richards mentioned the second name. He, however, felt a cold shock wave that went deep into the pit of his stomach. "Are you for real?" he asked, his mind reeling. If Richards was right, it would mean that Jessie had entangled herself in something much bigger than either of them ever imagined up to this point.

"Yes, Detective, I'm 'for real' and so is this court order." Richards showed him the document.

Jessie put a hand on his arm again. "Steve, do you understand what he's talking about?"

He struggled to decide where to begin. "I understand what he's saying. I'm not sure I believe what he's suggesting. And if he's right, Jessie, it may not be very good news for Laura."

"I wouldn't say that yet, Detective. I can't tell you everything I know, but if your mother is actually Paula Brandino we might have an explanation for your sister's disappearance."

Jessie looked at Steve, confusion written on her

face. "What's he saying? And which one of you is right about Laura?" She turned to Richards. "You need to explain yourself to me. This is my mother and my sister you're talking about, and I want to know exactly what you think is going on. And until I know I'm not giving my permission for anything."

Richards's expression hardened even more. "I don't need your permission, Ms. Barker. It would be helpful to have your approval but the court order is all I need to exhume the body. I can give you half an hour to try and explain this. After that I need to go to that cemetery and put this court order in motion."

"So let's go back in my office, Mr. Richards. I'm going to insist that Detective Gardner join us. He's been working this case from the beginning and he's kept me informed every step of the way. I think it's only fair that he should know whatever you have to tell me."

Richards's brow furrowed. "It's not the way I wanted to do things, but I'd be telling him most of this anyway. Come on back and I'll tell you as much as I can."

At least he was honest, Steve thought. The FBI agent didn't say he was going to tell them all he knew, even now at the beginning. This conversation was likely to produce even more pain and a lot of revelation for Jessie. It would be a good thing for him to be along. He began to gather his wits as they walked down the hall to Jessie's office. At the same time he started a fervent silent prayer. His own wits weren't going to be nearly enough to get them through the next half hour.

...

SEVEN

Steve looked tense. Jessie desperately wanted to get
him alone for just a minute or two and ask him
several questions. Should she really trust this FBI
agent? His identification looked real enough, and it
satisfied Steve. She didn't think the detective would
be easily fooled, so she wasn't worried about Agent
Richards being a fake. Still, she wasn't sure how
much to believe from him.

She felt a little more secure in her own office. It
was barely big enough to accommodate the two men
along with her. Usually it felt much larger than this,
but she only had one student at a time in here for
company during her office hours. The two law enforcement officers took up a bit more room than
most of her students, and neither of them wanted to
get too close to the other. Watching them settle
uneasily into the hard plastic chairs made Jessie

think of the big cats at the zoo, sizing each other up with steel between them. Both of the men sat in very upright positions, and the set of Steve's shoulders told her that he didn't totally trust the FBI agent. She hadn't seen enough of Joshua Richards yet to read all of his body language, but what she could read spelled wariness.

"All right, if we only have half an hour, you need to start talking, Mr. Richards," she told him. He seemed surprised at someone else directing the conversation; maybe that didn't happen for him every day. "First, help me understand a little bit more about the task force you're on. The initials OC don't mean anything to me."

"It's organized crime, Jessie," Steve broke in. "Do you know anything about that subject?"

"Not too much. There's a part of a chapter on the Mafia in my book, but mostly just dispelling the myths built up around gangsters and such due to Hollywood and a generation of novels."

Steve looked slightly puzzled and Richards downright confused. "I teach popular culture here at the community college," she explained to him, "and I've written a book about urban legends. It's called *A Friend of a Friend* because that's always who those stories happen to."

The light went on behind Richards's blue eyes.

"Ah. I should have done a little more background research on you. I'm afraid I've been concentrating on your mother first."

He sounded so sure that her mother was this person with a dual life. She took a deep breath and tried to organize her thoughts. "All right. What I've gathered so far is that you think you have reason to believe that my mother, Dawn Barker, also went by the name of Paula…"

"Brandino," the agent finished. "If you're not familiar with the workings of organized crime, that name may not mean much to you."

"It doesn't," Jessie admitted. "I have a feeling you're going to tell me, though."

The man's expression grew even more serious. "If you've written about urban legends, Ms. Barker, this is all going to sound like one of them to you. But I assure you it's the truth."

"That remains to be seen." Jessie settled more comfortably into her desk chair. She laced her fingers together on top of her desk, hoping she appeared professional and attentive. Inside she was just willing her hands not to shake while she listened to this man who might bring her world crashing down around her again. She looked over to Steve, hoping for a little comfort, but he looked as tense as she felt.

Joshua Richards might have been the most serious man Jessie had ever seen. Of course there wasn't much about the current situation to make anybody happy, but his lean face and prominent brow looked molded into a permanent expression of sternness. When she looked over at Steve his face mirrored Richards's in its expression and there was a tiny muscle twitch in his cheek.

"I'll try not to give you too much unnecessary history, but I have to give you some if you're not familiar with organized crime. Jake Brandino is the head of one of America's largest crime families. He's based out of Detroit and deals in gambling and money laundering, primarily. He took over the organization following his father's death from a heart attack and his uncle going to prison, events that took place over thirty years ago."

"What put his uncle behind bars?" Steve leaned back in his chair while Jessie wondered what difference it made when it happened before she was born.

"Jake's younger sister Paula had a gift for numbers, and even at twenty she was already being trained to be the family accountant. But she got caught buying drugs one night and ended up making the charges go away by offering to testify against her father and uncle."

Paula. That was what Richards had said was her

mother's other name. Jessie sat in her office in her familiar chair feeling stunned. Could the beautiful young woman she remembered as her mother have been involved in something like that? It really did sound like the stories she'd researched and debunked for her book.

Steve's voice broke into her thoughts. "If this Paula Brandino testified against her family that long ago then how did she last for thirty years? And what led you to believe that Paula is also Dawn Barker?"

Joshua gave Steve a sharp look that made Jessie feel as if neither of them remembered she was in the room. "You probably already know the answers to those questions. Why are you asking them?"

"Because Jessie doesn't know the answers. And I want to have her hear them from you up front."

Jessie could feel the muscles in her shoulders tense, and her temples tighten with an oncoming headache. "Now, look, the two of you. I don't know what's going on between you. If this is some kind of law enforcement one-upmanship I don't like being in the middle of it. This is my life we're talking about, and my mother whose memory you're maligning. I've got my own question for you, Mr. Richards. Is any of this going to help bring my sister back?"

Both men turned their attention on her. Richards's

steely gaze made Jessie shiver, while Steve looked as if he wanted to reach for her hand but didn't, probably out of propriety. "It's possible. If what I already believe is true, and I think it is, then proving that your mother was Paula Brandino could lead us to Laura."

"All right then, answer Steve's questions. How did Paula survive after testifying against her own family?"

"She was given a new identity, put into the witness security program. Most people refer to it as the Witness Protection program, but that's not what they called it during the eighties when Paula went into the program."

"Does it really work the way I've heard it does? You're given a new identity, and make no contact with anyone you knew before?"

Richards nodded. "That's the way it's supposed to work. Records from the federal marshals who administered the program are virtually impossible to come by. You can understand why, because revealing witnesses' new identities would put hundreds of people in jeopardy. But the FBI has been investigating about half a dozen deaths over the last three decades that involve people believed to be part of the program. All have organized crime ties and all were also involved with the same group of federal marshals."

Steve's expression grew even grimmer. "That doesn't sound good. Apparently you think Jessie's mother is linked to all of this or you wouldn't be here. And you definitely wouldn't have a court order to exhume her body."

"Can I do anything to contest that?" Jessie looked over at Steve, relatively sure she knew the answer to her question, but hoping that for once she was wrong.

"You might be able to delay him for a day or two. But ultimately he's probably going to be able to enforce his court order, Jessie." Steve looked away from her quickly, as if to show that he'd let her down. She felt like telling him that all of this wasn't his fault. If anything he'd been the one person to believe her when no one else had.

"Could you give me a little time to take all of this in, Mr. Richards? I'd like to at least request that you hold off until tomorrow if you could on executing your court order." Jessie stood behind her desk and both men rose, as well.

"I can wait until morning if I have to, Ms. Barker." Richards didn't look pleased but at least he didn't force the issue. "Let me leave you my number if you have any further questions today. I'll give a card to Detective Gardner, as well, since he's the person from the sheriff's department most familiar with the case already."

Steve took the card wordlessly, looking intensely at the federal agent while he laid a card on Jessie's desk, inclined his head slightly by way of a goodbye and walked out of her office. Steve watched the other man all the way down the hall. "You don't fully trust him, do you?" Jessie said softly once Richards was gone.

"Not totally. Some of it's just the antagonism between the local department and the bureau. They often find ways to make themselves unpopular when we cooperate with an investigation. Somehow the sharing of information between our department and the feds tends to be a one-way exchange."

"I can see why that would lead to some mistrust. Is there something more than that?"

Steve shrugged. "Nothing I could base on anything but feelings. I don't like the way that Richards conveniently appeared on this particular day. And I wish he'd involved somebody I knew from the bureau's St. Louis field office. It would have looked more like he was trying to go through channels that way."

"Can you check him out?"

"I can, and I will, just as soon as I make sure you're settled at home for the evening." Steve looked around the office. "Do you have more you absolutely have to do here? And once you go home, do you have anybody else you can call if you need company?"

Jessie sighed. "After all of this I can't concentrate anymore here. I don't know why I ever thought that coming back after the memorial service would be a good idea."

"Because you probably didn't want to go home and face a quiet place alone," Steve said, voicing her feelings so precisely that Jessie felt startled.

"You're right. And I have to admit I'm still not looking forward to it but I have to do it sometime. Why don't you walk me out to my car and I'll get going?"

She shut down her computer, gathered her tote bag full of books and papers and turned out the office lights. It seemed like a longer walk than usual out to the parking lot, even with Steve along. They were both quiet until they reached her car. "I'd go someplace with you, but I really need to get back and check out our friend Agent Richards. If there was a way to have you come back with me, I'd let you."

"That's all right. I know you'll tell me everything that you can if you find anything out."

Steve put a hand on her shoulder in a reassuring way. "You know I'll give you as much information as I can share as soon as I can. Now have a safe drive home. Do you want me to call you later?"

She looked up at his familiar face, noticing the tiny lines at the corners of his eyes. "I don't know. Who will be calling…the detective on my sister's case, or my friend Steve?"

He removed his hand and gave her a quiet smile. "A little bit of both. Most of what I did today was as the detective. Checking out Richards will be a job for both the detective and your friend. If he's legitimate he might be doing me a favor."

"What do you mean by that?" Jessie thought she might know the answer to her question already, but didn't want to jump to the wrong conclusion.

"I want to find Laura, but I also want my supervision of this case to be over. There's a strict department policy about not dating anyone involved in a case, and I don't want to go against that policy. It's there for very good reasons, all of which I understand. But I have to admit that for the first time in my life I've been tempted to stretch the boundaries of that policy with you."

"Wow. That's some admission from a man with such high standards. I think I should be flattered." Even though she hadn't had much to smile about today, she felt just a small smile pop up now.

"I guess so. But you didn't ever answer my question. Do you want me to call later?"

"Yes, I'd appreciate that. If you don't get me right

away, don't be alarmed. As odd as it sounds, I think I'm going to make a little detour on the way home and go to the animal shelter."

His expression looked as puzzled as she expected it might. "Okay. Hope you find what you're looking for."

"That will be interesting, because I'm not quite sure what I'm looking for. I just know I wouldn't mind having somebody to come home to."

"What will Laura think about that when she comes back?"

"She'd be thrilled. She's said for years that we needed an animal or two around the house. I've always been the holdout."

"Good luck, then. I'll call you later to see how it goes." He watched as she got into her car and closed the door. Jessie's last sight of him in the parking lot was of Steve standing there, a bemused expression on his face as she pulled out.

"I really was only going to look. You're not supposed to be coming home with me," Jessie chided the newest member of the Barker household. "At least you're not a puppy. My life just doesn't have room for a puppy right now. A mature individual like you I can probably handle." The little dog she watched in her rearview mirror had her tongue hanging out, looking quite a bit as though she was smiling.

Her trip to the animal shelter had been short. Walking in she promised herself that this would be the first of several scouting trips to decide if she really wanted a dog or not. Then the young volunteer at the front counter had her walk through the small dog area and she just couldn't get past the third cage. "Tell me about this one," she'd said, and the volunteer tilted her head thoughtfully.

"That's Maude. Her owner was an older lady and she passed on. Nobody in her family wanted Maude. We've tried her out in a couple situations. She's not great with very small children, and she doesn't care much for cats."

"That's okay. Neither do I." Maude's huge dark eyes regarded Jessie with something akin to understanding, and she sat down right in front of the cage door and gave one succinct bark, stubby tail thumping. "Can I see her up close?"

"Sure. Let me get a leash and you two can get acquainted." Jessie was still telling herself she was only looking. She was *not* going home with a dog. But Maude seemed to have other ideas. The moment she had the leash on she trotted out of the cage and plopped down directly in front of Jessie with an expression that said "Okay, let's go." After a moment she started walking toward the front of the shelter, giving another look over her shoulder when the leash started tugging.

"What is she, exactly?" Jessie asked as she filled out the paperwork to take Maude home.

"Um, that's a good question. Mostly corgi, we think. Nobody's totally sure, and the family didn't know, either. Her owner just referred to her as a 'pound puppy' because she'd been a rescue dog six years ago."

And she's a rescue dog again, Jessie thought. Only this time she was the one being rescued, from her too-quiet condo and the aching loneliness Laura's absence caused. "Laura's going to love you," she told Maude on the way home. For the first time in days Jessie felt real hope that she'd see her sister again, all because of a smiling dog. That night she slept better than she had in a month, even though the dog at the foot of the bed snored.

EIGHT

"Okay, when you said you were going by the animal shelter last night, I thought it was just going to be a scouting run." Steve looked through the window at the driver's seat of Jessie's car where Maude sat pertly, her tongue lolling in her trademark grin.

"Well, I didn't count on finding Maude. That's her name. And before you ask, I have no idea what she is besides part corgi and healthy. We've already been to the vet this morning and made friends, and we went to the pet supply store to buy a dog bed I suspect she'll never use."

Jessie couldn't believe how neatly Maude fit herself into her life so far. Having somebody else in the house, even though that "somebody" had four feet, changed her attitude overnight. She woke up feeling refreshed, and she talked to the little dog while she got ready for work. Then they went out for a quick walk and shared breakfast in the kitchen before making the stops she'd told Steve about.

His bemused smile said it all. "I hope she likes me. Because it looks like it may be a deal-breaker if she doesn't. What's the old saying? 'Love me, love my dog' I think."

Jessie pretended she hadn't heard the "love" part of that statement. After all, it was an expression. That's all it was, right? She opened the car door, taking the other end of the leash still attached to Maude's collar. "Come on, girl. Come meet Steve."

The dog jumped down to the ground and walked up to Steve somewhat warily. He must have had a dog sometime in his life, because he stood still, holding out the fingers of his hand near Maude, but not right in her face. She sniffed him and must have decided he passed the test because she gave his hand a quick lick then parked herself at Jessie's feet again. "Well, that's a relief. I didn't want to start out on her bad side."

"I'm not sure that would be possible unless you were mean to her. So far she acts like the sweetest girl I've ever seen. Laura is going to love her."

"I'm looking forward to meeting your sister, Jessie. She sounds as sweet as Maude here." The dog perked up at the mention of her name, and Steve reached down to scratch behind her ears.

"She is. I just wish we knew what was going on with her, where she is right now."

"If Richards is totally on the level, we may have a chance to find that out."

Jessie shook her head. "I'm not so sure I can believe that. It's hard for me to think he's right about my mother."

Steve straightened up from paying attention to the dog. "If he's right it would explain a lot. She's been someplace for almost twenty-five years. And if she has ties to a crime organization, there might be some reason that those same people abducted your sister."

Jessie found herself shuddering. "I don't know what's worse, believing that my mother was a criminal, or worrying that somebody like that has Laura."

"First Richards is going to have to provide his proof that his theory is more than just a theory. I have to admit that they may be hard to work with, but the FBI doesn't usually go off on a wild-goose chase. If Richards is pushing this idea, he has something to back it up already."

"Is there any way I can fight his court order?" The little bit of research she'd been able to do the night before told Jessie it was unlikely.

"You could try, but it wouldn't stick permanently. You'd only be postponing the inevitable." Steve's eyes searched her face. "Is fighting the court order worth anything? The up side to giving Richards his way quickly is that if he's right, we might be closer to finding Laura."

In the end that mattered more than the rest of it. "I'm going to take Maude with me and drive over to the cemetery. I won't stay there for long, but I feel like I should be there for a short while."

"I'll meet you there. I'd offer to ride over together but I need to be there officially and I don't think that includes putting a dog in the department vehicle unless it's a K-9 corps animal." Steve looked a little sheepish. "I think she'd be just fine, but let's not force the issue and get any of us in trouble."

As if she understood, Maude gave a short bark that made them both laugh. Jessie felt very thankful that she'd stopped at the animal shelter. Anything that could make this incredibly difficult day even a little bit easier was a good thing. "I should have done this a long time ago," she told Maude. "But then I might have ended up with somebody else that wouldn't be nearly as cute as you." The stubby tail thumped the ground again and Jessie led Maude back to the car.

When Jessie got to the cemetery Joshua Richards was already there along with employees with heavy equipment and a second person dressed in white work coveralls. Richards looked surprised to see Jessie there. "All right, I knew Detective Gardner was coming, but I figured you'd use him as a representative. This is not going to be a pleasant process, and it's not one that most family members choose to witness."

"I won't be staying long, Agent Richards. I just wanted to tell you that although I can't convince myself that my mother is really Paula Brandino, I'm not going to try and stop your investigation, either."

"That's good. You wouldn't have much success in stopping it anyway. My task force has pretty high priority, and that court order I got will stick." Richards looked as if he was going to say more, but then he stopped, looking over Jessie's shoulder. "Ms. Barker, there seems to be a dog driving your car."

Jessie looked back with him. "Oh, that's just Maude. I adopted her yesterday and she still wants to be everywhere I am. And she's not driving, just sitting in the driver's seat until I get back. I have the keys and she can't shift the car out of Park without them. I already checked."

The agent still couldn't take his eyes off Maude. "Good. And if you don't mind, I'll have to ask you to keep her in the car."

"Are you afraid she'll jeopardize the investigation somehow?"

Richards shook his head. "Only my health. I'm very allergic to animal dander."

"I'll keep her there, then," Jessie told him as she fought the temptation to do just the opposite. "Going back to your investigation…Steve tells me that he thinks you might be able to help us find Laura if you're right."

"I'm right. We just need Kyra to prove it," Richards said, motioning toward the young woman in coveralls. She must have heard her name because she walked over to join them. "Kyra Elliott, this is Jessie Barker. Her mother is the focus of our investigation."

Kyra seemed young. Jessie wondered if she were truly as youthful as her unlined, fresh face looked and if so what she could be doing here in charge of anything. Either her thoughts must have shown on her face, or Kyra was extremely perceptive. "I'm doing postgraduate work in forensic medicine at the most reputable program in the nation. That's why the FBI uses me in cases like this. It's actually *Dr.* Elliott if you want to check me out."

Her green eyes flashed with challenge and her chin thrust out as if Kyra was used to defending herself. Jessie thought that she might look even younger and less like a Ph.D. if her coppery hair were hanging loose instead of caught up tightly at the back of her head.

"I'm not here to question your credentials, Dr. Elliott. In fact I am happy to hear that if this has to be done the FBI uses an expert. I just don't think you're going to find what you hope to." Jessie paused for a moment. "I guess if I'm honest I just don't want you to be right. It's hard enough to deal with my mother walking away from us all those years ago. To think that she might be a criminal, as well, is difficult to handle."

The other woman's eyes lost their challenging look. "I can only imagine what you must be going through. I'm sorry for your loss. We'll see that you're kept as informed as possible once I find out what I can."

"And how long do you think that will take?" Jessie didn't really expect an answer, but Kyra had been so open so far she gave it a try.

"Most of the tests I'll do will take a few hours apiece. But some of the tissue matching and other work take up to a week. There's very little room for error in the tests I do. Once we have our results there will be almost no question about the identity of this woman."

"That's good to know. I don't know whether to hope that you find what you're looking for or that you don't. My mother's reputation might be slightly better, but then we're no closer to finding Laura."

"I think that's more important than just proving the identity of a dead woman." Kyra paused. "I didn't mean that as any disrespect to your mother, Ms. Barker. That's the last thing I'd do. In my job I feel like I'm the last spokesperson for the dead."

Jessie swallowed hard. "That's a big responsibility."

"I couldn't do it alone. And I want to reassure you that once I'm done with my tests everything concerning your mother will be put back here to your satisfaction."

"Thank you." This woman was treating her with dignity and concern. After the events of the last few weeks, Jessie wasn't surprised by the tiny gold cross she could see at the neck of Kyra's jumpsuit. She must have been focusing on it, because Kyra glanced down, her cheeks flushed slightly. Quickly she reflexively zipped up the garment. She didn't say anything more, just dismissively shrugged one shoulder.

"I try not to wear jewelry during a job like this, because it's just one more thing that could possibly transfer something foreign into the scene. I almost never take this off, though, and it slipped my mind. It will be okay if I keep it totally covered. It won't affect the investigation."

Jessie tried to hide a smile. "I think it already has,

but not in a way I'd argue with." Kyra's answering smile showed she understood what Jessie meant.

Once Steve got there Jessie was more than happy to turn things over to him. "This is going to be kind of rough, even for me. But I'm bound to be here anyway as the department's representative on the case. I'll just be your representative, as well." He gave her a quick hug.

"And I thank you for it. I think Maude and I are going to go do some computer research. Maybe I can get some proof that my mother wasn't the criminal you all suggest that she is."

Steve's brow wrinkled. "Now don't put me totally in that camp. I'm keeping an open mind until they produce the hard evidence."

"Sounds like a detective's argument. I'll just keep holding the thought that perhaps this will get us closer to finding Laura."

"That's the hope, Jessie. I'll keep you posted." Jessie wasn't sure she wanted to trust Richards and his testing, but she knew that whatever happened she could trust Steve to do the right thing.

Cassidy stood in the cemetery again, furtively looking for anyone who resembled a groundskeeper. Only someone who was here frequently and quite astute would have connected today's disguise with the family member tidying a grave before. Patrick's last message had been concise and terse. He left little to the imagination regarding what should be done with Jessica Barker.

"I can't do anything right away," Cassidy had told him. "It would look too strange. Suicidal people don't go out and adopt a pet."

"So find a way around it. Kill the dog first. Gates get left open all the time, and dogs get out."

"And losing a beloved pet, even a new one, could push someone over the edge during a hard time. It has possibilities," Cassidy told him, thinking on the idea.

"Don't take too much time. I know you too well, Cassidy. Patience isn't your strong suit."

"I can't deny that." Now Cassidy watched the forensic expert, cursing the luck that brought even more people into the picture to complicate things. Getting close enough to kill Jessica Barker without scaring her off wasn't going to be easy.

Even Maude wasn't much comfort once Jessie started getting deeper into her Internet research. She hoped Steve had more luck checking out Joshua Richards because there was precious little online that a regular person could access about the FBI's agents and personnel.

Now the task force Richards was part of was an entirely different story. Jessie learned plenty about organized crime from the FBI Web site; so much in fact that she grabbed a lined pad of paper and started jotting down questions for the FBI agent. Given the scope of the bureau's fight against that type of crime there had to be half a dozen task forces like the one Richards was part of, and they all focused on a different kind of organized crime from a different part of the world.

Jessie felt even more downhearted once she started looking at the Brandino crime family in detail. They were a real, viable presence within the network of Italian-American families running a lot of the drug, money laundering and illegal firearms schemes in the country. To make things even more complicated and depressing, organized crime these days wasn't limited to people of any one ethnic background. Groups from all over the world came to America to tap the country's vast resources for illegal purposes.

Jessie's head spun. There were too many things to look at, and unfortunately her mother being connected with this Brandino family sounded more reasonable the more she looked into the nature of organized crime. At first she'd rejected the idea outright, but then her brain had started to work.

Being part of an organized crime family wasn't any more repellent than having an affair with someone with criminal ties, and she'd been willing to believe that. What was all this like twenty-four years ago? And who could tell her about that?

"Come on, you're a college instructor. You can figure this out," Jessie muttered. The biggest problem was that if Richards was right, she had a reason for her mother leaving them, but what a reason. And it still meant that her father and some nameless woman died in that car crash that her mother walked away from, just as she walked away from her children.

"Mom, what did you do?" she murmured. Tears came to her eyes and her hands on the keyboard trembled. It was all too much. All of a sudden she didn't want to know. She didn't want to know *any* of this and she didn't want to talk to anybody connected with this whole mess. She just wanted to have a little peace in her life, but even that wasn't possible because her sister was still missing and so far nobody could do anything about that.

She brushed her face with the back of one hand, trying not to totally break down. Maude whined softly and pawed Jessie's leg. "I want to go home, too," she told the little dog. She turned off the computer and put it in her bag to take with her, along with the pad and pen she'd been using for her notes. Walking out of the office she noticed that Mrs. Turner was still there.

"You're here awfully late," Jessie remarked. The middle-aged woman smiled, and Jessie realized she hadn't seen her do that very much. She hadn't exchanged that many words with the woman outside of discussing department-related issues. She kept her desk very neat, with a couple of small pictures that were probably family members in frames near the computer.

"There were things to catch up on, and nobody is waiting for me at home, so I figured it would be a good time to do them." She looked as if she was in the process of getting ready to leave, as well. "What about you? I don't think you have any evening classes this semester, do you, Dr. Barker?"

"Please, it's Professor Barker or just plain Ms. Barker. No Ph.D. yet." Getting her master's degree in history had been enough when she was in her early twenties and worried how to support them both until Laura finished school. "So if we're both at loose ends tonight, would you like to grab dinner somewhere? You've been working here over a month and I haven't really gotten to know you at all. That's not the way I usually operate."

"I can tell that. The other instructors in the department have remarked on how all your troubles in the last few weeks have changed your normal habits. Not in a gossipy way, mind you. They seem concerned about you." Mrs. Turner's computer turned off, and she slid her rolling chair away from the desk. "But if we're going to go to dinner together, first off you'll have to call me Linda. And I suppose you're going to need a few minutes extra time to get somebody settled at home." She looked down at Maude, who cocked her head and took a step backward.

"I suppose I will," Jessie said. They discussed local restaurants and chose one closer to her condo that Linda said wasn't out of her way. "Why don't you go hold us a table and have a coffee or something while I take Maude home and join you?"

Linda nodded and Jessie felt her heart lift just a little. It was interesting to have somebody to talk to who was probably close to the age of her mother. And maybe Linda could answer some of her questions about what life in general had been like over twenty-five years ago for someone in their twenties then. It wouldn't give her any insight into organized crime, but it might give her more of a feeling for the time in general. Jessie had something new to think about all the way home.

NINE

"So, did you get your puppy all settled?" Linda Turner looked up from the menu she was reading in the restaurant booth. The place was a chain dinner house Jessie didn't go to often but it was a good place to talk without calling any attention to oneself and the food would be decent and predictable. Tonight that all sounded fine.

"She's not really a puppy." Jessie slid into her side of the booth. "In fact I got her because she was older and already trained. Even on my best days I don't have the time and energy for training a puppy."

"And from what I hear there haven't been many of those best days for you recently anyway." Linda looked pleasant and motherly. "Just the parade of law enforcement officers through your office would be enough to rattle most people. Are they helping you any or just hounding you? My ex-husband was a cop and I don't trust them to do the best thing all the time." Her nose wrinkled in distaste. "They have their own agenda all too often."

Jessie wanted to argue that they weren't all that way. Steve at least was different, but the words stayed on her tongue. She and Steve may have made a connection, but he was still the detective on her mother and sister's case. In some ways he had to have his own agenda to stay focused on his job. "I guess you're right."

"I'm sure some of them are better than others. That young man from the county sheriff's department seems all right I suppose. But that other one…" Linda almost shivered. "He's got such cold eyes."

They were pale blue at least, Jessie thought. He wasn't always the friendliest individual, either; sometimes she felt as though he was observing her a little too closely. Maybe her discomfort around Joshua Richards wasn't just a fluke. Before she said anything the server was there to take their order and once that was over it felt like time to start a new subject instead of this rather grim one.

Jessie thought for a moment about how to approach what she wanted to know without offending Linda. Without any real experience talking to women her mother's age about their past and things

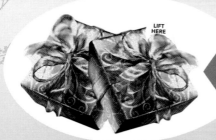

W

e'd like to send you two free books to introduce you to the Love Inspired® Suspense series. Your two books have a combined c price of $9.98 in the U.S. and $11.98 in Canada, but they are yours We'll even send you two wonderful surprise gifts. You can't lose!

Each of your **FREE** books is filled with riveting inspirational suspense featuring Christian characters facing challenges to faith...and their lives

GET 2 FREE BOOKS!

HURRY!
Return this card promptly to get 2 FREE Books and 2 FREE Bonus Gifts!

YES! Please send me the **2 FREE Love Inspired® Suspense books** and **2 FREE gifts** for which I qualify. I understand that I am under no obligation to purchase anything further, as explained on the back of this card.

Love Inspired®
SUSPENSE
RIVETING INSPIRATIONAL ROMANCE

PLACE FREE GIFTS SEAL HERE

◄ DETACH AND MAIL CARD TODAY! ►

LISUS-IV-07

323 IDL EL5D   123 IDL EL4D

FIRST NAME

LAST NAME

ADDRESS

APT.#   CITY

STATE/PROV.   ZIP/POSTAL CODE

Steeple Hill®

Offer limited to one per household and not valid to current subscribers of Love Inspired® Suspense books.

Your Privacy – Steeple Hill Books is committed to protecting your privacy. Our Privacy Policy is available online at www.SteepleHill.com or upon request from the Steeple Hill Reader Service™. From time to time we make our lists of customers available to reputable firms who may have a product or service of interest to you. If you would prefer for us not to share your name and address, please check here. ☐

Steeple Hill Reader Service™ — Here's How It Works:

Accepting your 2 free books and 2 free gifts places you under no obligation to buy anything. You may keep the books and gifts and return the shipping statement marked "cancel." If you do not cancel, about a month later we'll send you 4 additional books and you just $3.99 each in the U.S. or $4.74 each in Canada, plus 25¢ shipping & handling per book and applicable taxes if any.* Th the complete price and — compared to cover prices of $4.99 each in the U.S. and $5.99 each in Canada — it's quite a bargain! may cancel at any time, but if you choose to continue, every month we'll send you 4 more books, which you may either purchas the discount price or return to us and cancel your subscription.

*Terms and prices subject to change without notice. Sales tax applicable in N.Y. Canadian residents will be charged applicable provincial t and GST. All orders subject to approval. Books received may vary. Credit or debit balances in a customer's account(s) may be offset by any o outstanding balance owed by or to the customer. Please allow 4 to 6 weeks for delivery.

If offer card is missing write to: Steeple Hill Reader Service, 3010 Walden Ave., P.O. Box 1867, Buffalo, NY 14240-1867

BUSINESS REPLY MAIL

FIRST-CLASS MAIL   PERMIT NO. 717-003   BUFFALO, NY

POSTAGE WILL BE PAID BY ADDRESSEE

STEEPLE HILL READER SERVICE
3010 WALDEN AVE
PO BOX 1867
BUFFALO NY 14240-9952

NO POSTAGE
NECESSARY
IF MAILED
IN THE
UNITED STATES

that brought up their age it was hard to know where to begin. She remembered the photos on Linda's desk and decided to start there. "I saw the pictures on your desk. Are those your family?"

Linda nodded. "Yes, but I'm afraid neither of them is quite current. Teddy and Amy are both in college now. I suppose I should tell them I want new pictures for Christmas. Those high-school senior shots just don't do them justice. Kids have a way of becoming adults on you in a heartbeat." Her smile was that of a loving parent proud of her kids, and it gave Jessie a momentary stab of pain.

She took a deep breath and decided to be open with Linda. "If you've been talking to the other instructors, then you know that not only did I bury my mom this week, but that she and I were estranged, to say the least. I've really been trying to figure out why she would have walked out on two small children the way she did. If you've got kids who are in college, it's likely you were a young mom in your twenties just a few years after my mom was going through the same thing."

Linda sat back against the high padded booth. "Yes, I guess I was. What are you looking for, Ms. Barker?"

"Please, if I'm supposed to call you Linda, you have to call me by my first name, too. Outside of the office I'm definitely Jessie. If you want to be formal when we're both at work then that's up to you. But here, it's Jessie."

"All right then. The question's still the same. What are you trying to find out, Jessie?"

She leaned her chin on one cupped hand, trying to find the right words. "Nothing particular and everything all at once. I guess I'm trying to get a feel for what it must have been like for my mom twenty-five years ago, staying at home raising two little kids while my dad worked long hours as the lowest guy in the food chain at a state college out in the boonies."

Linda gave a short, wry laugh. "I can relate to that. Twenty years ago I was in a similar situation, except as I mentioned before, my husband was a beat cop, a patrolman. We had plenty of long hours, lots of stress and not all that much money. We divorced when the children were barely out of diapers and then things really got stressful."

"Did you share custody of the kids?" Jessie wasn't sure why that question came out the way it did, but she wanted to know.

"Not for long. Their father was killed during a robbery about five years after we divorced. He was moonlighting as security at a shopping mall, supposedly to pay child support but where that money really went I'll never know. We got by but it wasn't easy." She looked down at the table a moment as if to collect herself and then patted her short graying strawberry blonde hair into place. "But I imagine that wasn't the kind of thing you were asking about."

"Oddly enough, I think it was. I know just from teaching my pop culture units that the eighties weren't exactly a feminist stronghold of total equality. Women who built careers and wore power suits garnered a lot more respect than the ones who stayed home with little kids."

The older woman nodded. For a moment Jessie caught a flash of something in her eyes that might have been anger or disappointment, but it was gone quickly. And then the server was back with their salads and the table fell silent for a while. As she pushed the lettuce around, Jessie tried to use what Linda had said and put herself in her mother's position almost a quarter-century before. Even without adding a crime family into the situation, it didn't feel like a comfortable place to be.

They ate in silence for a little while and then Linda cleared her throat softly. "I don't want you to think life was all terrible back then. Some of it was good, especially with the kids. And I don't regret having them."

Not like my mother did, Jessie thought, the

strength of her conviction shocking her into continued silence. She had few memories of her mother, but
none of them involved those things some of her
friends talked about, such as spontaneous ice-cream
cones, finger painting at the kitchen table or making
floury messes baking cookies together. Even the
picture she had of that one lone picnic came about
because her father insisted on going, and taking the
picture.

Across the table, Linda seemed to be waiting for
her to say something. "I can't imagine you regret-
ting the time spent raising your kids. And I bet it
shows now that they're adults themselves."

That was all the leeway Linda needed to talk
about Ted and Amy for most of the rest of the meal,
leaving Jessie to wonder how good an idea this had
been. In the end she decided it was worthwhile even
though it had been painful, because seeing Linda
had made her reach back into her own past to
confront the reality of the mother she truly remembered instead of some fantasy mother out of a TV
sitcom. When she went home to Maude later that
evening she was happy just to stay there with the
dog, bonding with her while ignoring the flash of the
answering machine's messages. The world, including Steve Gardner, would still be there when she felt
like rejoining it.

On Fridays Jessie didn't have classes to teach after noon, so she went in, lectured for her morning students and went to the main location of the St. Charles county library. There was more information online these days than in books on many subjects, but she still liked the feel of a book. It was a rainy day and spending the afternoon reading and researching was satisfying. All of this made Jessie think of her grad school days, except that the stakes here were a little higher in this research.

She still hadn't listened to any of the messages on her home machine and that was okay with her. She wanted the chance to form her own opinions right now without interference from law enforcement. Linda's statement about the police "having their own agenda" echoed in Jessie's mind and she found it hard to dispute today.

Dinner that evening was a bowl of soup in front of the flickering gas log fire in the living room of the condo while she and Maude dried out after a damp walk in the light rain outside. The phone rang while she ate but Jessie didn't pick it up, letting the machine get it. When she heard Steve's voice she almost changed her mind. "I hope you're okay, Jessie. Call me when you can, just to tell me things are all right. I'm getting a little worried."

"He didn't say anything about making progress

in the case, did he?" Maude's tail thumped on the rug as Jessie talked to her. She decided that she'd call Steve back before she went to bed just to reassure him that she wasn't in trouble. Gathering the dinner dishes she took them into the kitchen and tidied up.

By now she'd learned about all she could from the books stacked around her chair and it was time to grab her laptop and start cruising different Web sites. She had marked places in several books and now went back to those spots to use the information as a starting point for more specific research.

When she started looking at Web sites she promised herself she'd only continue her research for an hour or two and then make an early night of it. This felt like one of the longest weeks of her life and she needed a good night's sleep. But one site led to another and then she found information that stopped her in her tracks. For two hours after that she alternated between Web sites and the books around her, trying to convince herself she hadn't really seen what she thought she had.

It was one o'clock on Saturday morning before she admitted defeat; the image she'd found hours before reappeared too much to be coincidence or mistake. She let Maude out briefly, drying the little dog off when she came back in out of the rain. Jessie struggled trying to decide whether to call Steve at this time of night or wait until morning.

Waiting definitely wouldn't be for her benefit because after what she'd found, tonight would be nightmare laden at best. Finally she decided that she couldn't wake him up this late after ignoring him for two days. She would call at a more reasonable hour on Saturday morning and hope that he paid more attention to her than she'd been paying to him.

Steve stood at Jessie's door, holding a bag of warm cinnamon rolls and a carrier with two coffee cups. Just about the time he started worrying that she wasn't answering the door, it opened. "Sorry about that. I put Maude in the kitchen so that she wouldn't run out. I don't think she's very car smart."

"Then it's a good thing you put her in there. She's been such a blessing for you that I'd hate to see anything happen to her." He handed her the bag of rolls. "I brought us a late breakfast. I figured you might not have much in the house."

Jessie smiled briefly. "You figured right. There hasn't been any time to do grocery shopping this week. Thanks for thinking of me." They went into the kitchen and sat at the table, Maude dancing around their legs begging for food and attention.

Jessie sighed. She looked worn, and behind her glasses he could see shadows under her eyes.

He wasn't sure how to be tactful about what he wanted to ask. Usually he dealt with suspects when he was asking questions, not friends. Diving right in felt like the right thing to do. "Okay, what's up? I've been thinking about you a lot. And calling you a fair amount, too. Do we have a problem?"

Jessie looked down at the plates she set out on the table for their rolls. "No, Steve we don't have a problem. I have several problems but most of them aren't yours. I needed some time to sort things out for myself. I got the time, but not the results I was hoping for."

When she looked up again her eyes brimmed with tears. "My mother really was Paula Brandino. I don't even have to wait for the tests that Kyra's doing for the proof. I found enough evidence by myself to know."

"How? You've been sitting in this condo for a day and a half now. What could you have found that way that gave you the proof you wouldn't take from Richards?"

Jessie's hands were trembling. "Pictures, Steve. I found pictures of the crime boss, Jake Brandino. And I recognized him. He's the man that was in charge of things the night my mother disappeared."

Steve sat back in his chair. This was the last thing he expected. Still, he felt thankful that Jessie had come to this recognition on her own because it would make some of what he needed to break to her a little easier. With someone else he might ask if she was sure, but Jessie, with her determination, was the wrong one for that question. "I'm sorry, for your sake. That had to be a shock."

"It was. In some ways it was proof that I hadn't imagined things all those years ago. After almost every adult in my life trying to tell me that nothing I remember from that night was real, this feels like vindication. Of course there's no way to prove anything to anyone else, but I know for sure now that it happened. That's worth a lot."

"And if we accept that the Brandino family has a lot of personal reasons to be involved in all this, I think I'd have to agree with Richards. There's something I didn't think I'd be admitting. But if your mother was Paula Brandino, then we have a solid lead to try and trace Laura."

Jessie nodded. "That's what I think, too. It's the reason I called you as early as I did. I almost tried at one in the morning when I figured this out, but I didn't want to wake you. If it had waited this long it could wait another few hours."

Steve felt touched that she'd thought of him as

a person instead of just an investigator. "That was kind of you. But I wouldn't have minded a call for something this important. I am grateful for the extra sleep. Since we're both somewhat rested, let's have breakfast and then get back to work on this. There's more new information to add to what you've found."

"Is it good news?" Jessie put a hand on her chest as if she felt her heart flutter.

Okay, how did he phrase this one? "It's different and surprising. And in the long run it probably is good news. But to tell the truth, Jessie, I need some of that coffee and something to eat before I get any deeper into any of this."

"Sorry. I'm letting it all get cold." They put rolls on plates and breakfasted in silence, with Jessie looking as eager to jump at him as Maude did. The difference was that the dog only wanted the crumbs from the cinnamon rolls and Jessie would be much harder to satisfy. She gave him the impression of a little kid at the other side of the table gauging just how little she could get away with eating and still call it breakfast.

Steve decided to eat his roll and enjoy the hot coffee while it was still hot. It might be a while before he got to have a meal with Jessie again in comfortable surroundings, so he'd make the best of it now.

After about five minutes Jessie had consumed about a fourth of her coffee and dissected the roll into pieces. She might have even eaten a few of the pieces. "All right, why don't you tell me what you know while you finish breakfast?" She leaned forward in expectation.

"You said what you found was pictures, right? And I have to assume they're on the computer since you haven't left the house." Jessie's eyes narrowed a little suspiciously. "What I've got is also stuff it would be easier to show you. Give me five more minutes and we'll look at pictures on our computers together. In fact, why don't you call up your information while I finish my coffee? That way you'll have something to do."

"And instead of pestering you and hounding you to hurry, I can bring up the information."

"Well, I wouldn't have put it quite that way, but yeah." Steve knew he had a sheepish smile, and to his surprise she answered him with a small smile. She went and got the laptop and started tinkering with it while he savored just a little more hot coffee before they got down to business.

In another few minutes he was looking at twenty-year-old pictures of Jake Brandino. Unlike the later pictures he'd seen that showed a man with a thickening waistline and gray at his temples, the shots that

Jessie had found showed a man in his prime with broad shoulders and slim hips and an aura of power about him already. Steve was struck by his resemblance to some of the things he needed to show Jessie, and silently thanked God that she'd found all of this on her own.

Grabbing his laptop out of his car he brought it in and showed Jessie first the shots of the Brandino family compound in a posh suburban enclave of Detroit. "As you can see, this is secluded. Brandino and his actual family members don't come out often. There's FBI and other federal surveillance pictures that can be tapped into, and that other wealth of information, tabloid journalism."

He watched her face as he called up the second file. "Now I know that these shots are a little blurry but they're the best I've been able to find. Once we get done here maybe we can convince your friend Joshua Richards to produce some better pictures."

Recognition didn't dawn immediately and he started narrating to go along with the pictures. "This is a group of family members leaving the compound in a car. I'm pretty sure the blond woman in the back is your mother."

Jessie peered at the screen. "When was this?"

"About six months ago. The driver is probably a bodyguard."

"And the other man in the front seat?"

Steve took a deep breath and let it out slowly. "Brandino's nephew, Matteo. The best information available says the kid is his heir apparent."

Jessie stared in silence for a while and he watched the expressions behind her blue-gray eyes change. "Have I missed something in the family tree? Because everything I've found so far tells me there were two Brandino siblings, Jake and Paula. Any more I don't know about?" Her expression pleaded with him to say that yes, there was a third brother or sister.

Steve shook his head. "Not to my knowledge. Research I've done so far is the same as yours."

"Okay. Why is the nephew next in line? Isn't Jake married?"

"No. He was married briefly as a young man, but the woman died without ever providing him with children."

"Then that guy in the front seat…" Jessie trailed off but Steve knew she'd figured it all out now. "How old is he, Steve?"

"Twenty-four. Your brother Matteo is twenty-four, Jessie. And all he's ever known is life behind those compound walls as a Brandino." She took it better than he thought she would. At least this time the shock didn't make Jessie pass out.

TEN

Jessie let her coffee get cold and ignored the rest of her cinnamon roll, even the icing. If Steve had known her better, these things alone would have told him how unnerved she was. Even without any appetite at all, passing up cinnamon and vanilla in the same package was pretty different for her. She was glad that he hadn't gotten that close yet. She wasn't sure how much of her feelings she felt ready to bare to him.

To cover her unease she started tidying up the kitchen. There were dozens of questions running through her head. "I have a brother," she mused. "I wonder what he's like. Do you think he enjoys being part of this Brandino family? Does he know that his mother's dead? And how much does he care? I mean, if I had grown up having a mother around all the time, then I found out something had happened to her I'd be there no matter what."

"You probably would." Steve looked thoughtful as he brought plates over to the sink. "I'd do the same thing. But you have to remember that your brother isn't exactly like you and me. With somebody like Matteo Brandino you have to take into consideration that if he's that deeply involved with an organized crime family, they might not let him go this far to see his mother."

She hadn't considered that before. "You mean he might know about it, but be kept from coming? That would be worse than not caring."

"I think so. And we don't know for sure yet who killed her and why. If Jake Brandino was the one who abducted your sister and Adrian Bando and ordered your mother's death then he's not going to let somebody as important to him as Matteo be anywhere near all that."

There was something Steve wasn't telling her; even from the short time she'd known him, Jessie could tell that. But she had so many new things on her mind right now that she hated to add one more problem. For the present she decided not to press the issue of what else Steve knew. So far he'd been more trustworthy than anybody else in this strange series of events. When he was able to share what he knew, he'd tell her.

Thinking of everybody involved made Jessie

come back to a previous idea. "We need to get together with Agent Richards again. If you found all of this through the FBI's organized crime task force, then he's probably known it all along. That's why he was so adamant about getting the proof that my mother was who he said she was. I want to find out what else he knows."

"Or at least as much as he'll tell us." Steve's usually generous mouth thinned as he pressed his lips together. "I think if we lay out for him everything we know already, he'll give us a fair amount of information. At least I hope so. I still don't like the guy much, but that may just be a personal thing without much basis."

"Why do you say that?" Jessie thought she saw more color creep up from Steve's collar. Possibly in an effort to disguise that, he busied himself breaking a few tiny bits off of her discarded roll and put them in Maude's dish. He definitely caused a distraction, and gained the dog's undivided attention. Jessie just gave him the same look she gave students who went silent on her until he answered. It worked better on freshmen than it did on Steve.

"Because I don't think I like the way he looks at you. It's as if he's assessing you somehow. And the way he looks doesn't strike me as just professional curiosity. I mean, I know you probably get your share of attention from all kinds of guys, but I'm not sure I like you getting it from him."

Now it was Jessie's turn to feel the flush of surprise warming her face. "It's very kind of you to say that, but it's hard for me to believe you mean it. Laura has always been the one in the family who's gotten the attention from men. Most guys see her and forget I'm in the room."

"Then they're not looking hard enough." Steve's voice was firm. "There are a lot of things to notice and like about you, Jessie. You catch on quickly and your passions shine in those flashing gray eyes."

When had he gotten so much closer? Jessie hadn't noticed his moving closer, she was so caught up in his words. They stood together on the rag rug in front of her kitchen sink, a decidedly unromantic location, while Steve said the most wonderful things she'd ever heard from a man. His hand traveled gently to her shoulder and she felt no urge to pull away.

"I know I'm not beautiful, Steve. I don't even believe that myself. Some of it is the glasses," she said, trying not to stammer. "And my plain brown hair. Laura's always after me to get a more current style, and maybe some highlights."

"As if nature hasn't already provided those." His voice was low and a little husky and his fingers brushed the ends of the hair he talked about, sending a slight shiver up her spine. "She probably brings up contact lenses, too, doesn't she?"

Jessie nodded. "That or laser surgery. But I'm just a little leery of having a surgeon correct a problem I can fix with glasses." Why was she rambling like this? Steve brought out things in her that made her feel like an awkward teenager again. Although no one like Steve had ever graced her teen years.

"That sounds incredibly sensible. Besides, if you had laser surgery or contact lenses, I wouldn't be able to anticipate this and believe me, I've been anticipating it." He gently, slowly slid her glasses off her face and put them on the kitchen counter. With no barrier between them, Stephen's dark eyes were slightly out of focus until he lowered his head close to hers. "For a while now I've wanted to take you in my arms, Jessie. At first it was just to comfort you with all these rotten things going on in your life. Later I wanted to do this for different reasons."

He was close enough now that she could pick out every emerald spark in his eyes. "If you want me to stop, now's the time to say something, Jessie."

She didn't want him to stop so she said nothing. Then when he paused so close to her that she could smell the cinnamon on his breath she wondered if she should stay silent. "What should I say if I don't want you to stop?" she said in a voice so low it was nearly a whisper.

"What you just said is fine." He closed the gap between them and sought out her lips. His were like velvet, insistent yet gentle. He didn't linger there or force any attention on her. Still, she found it hard to regain her equilibrium when he drew back. Steve's breathing seemed to mirror her own, slightly uneven. "I think you ought to put those back on," he said, solemnly handing her back the glasses.

"I think you're right." For somebody who spent hours every week lecturing entire classrooms of college students, Jessie found herself totally lacking for words.

"You know, it might be a good idea if we got out more. After that I think seeing each other in a more public place would be a good idea for a little while." Even with her glasses back on, Steve's eyes looked a little unfocused, but this time Jessie knew that was because of his own bemusement. He seemed as affected by their brief kiss as she did.

"What did you have in mind?"

"Rachel and Tom's wedding is coming up soon, and she's been after me to bring you ever since she met you. What do you think?"

Jessie thought that going to something as emotionally charged as that with Steve might be as difficult as being in her kitchen alone with him, but she didn't want to say that. Instead she agreed to go. "There's another public place we need to go together even sooner."

Steve stepped back a bit. "If you're talking about seeing Agent Richards, I think you need to do that alone. I don't want him to get the idea that our personal lives and the case are so tangled up together that he has a problem with either of us."

"Okay." Steve's decision left her feeling a little alone, but Jessie didn't share that, either. Being the only one handling a problem wasn't a new situation for her, just a disappointing one.

Cassidy was in a foul mood, tired of lurking in shadows in a mundane outpost of civilization that had nothing to recommend itself, including the weather. Of course, the one advantage to being in a nondescript suburb was that nobody paid any attention as long as you fit in.

It was easy to keep an eye on Jessica when she was at home. All Cassidy had to do was put on a familiar uniform. Posing as a service provider made you invisible.

Cassidy had learned that little other disguise was necessary for most people. A different hairstyle or colored contact lenses, perhaps, but that was really for personal satisfaction. Most people weren't observant enough to be worth the effort.

Jessica Barker had no idea how difficult she was being. Cassidy fantasized about telling her that before the end. At least she'd understand why she had to die a slow death. The woman was so careful and methodical, and that detective showed up constantly. Cassidy mulled over an anonymous way to report him to his supervisors so they wouldn't be together so much. Of course what they were doing had to be related to the case; the woman was too plain to be attractive to any man with real taste. Still, Cassidy knew that if the sheriff's department thought one of their detectives was guilty of improper conduct they might pull him off the case while they investigated.

That could provide another disappointment for Ms. Barker, one in this long series she'd faced. Surely they could add up to where she'd be unable to bear them. At least that could be the conclusion when she started her car in a closed garage, or overdosed on sleeping pills. With someone as isolated as Jessica, Cassidy could even fake a prescription. A few too many pills with a drink or two would do the trick.

Cassidy chafed at the restrictions until that could happen. Pretending to be interested in dull people, while keeping track of the Barker woman felt like a tiresome charade. Cassidy counted the days until the job would be over, dreaming of going back to regular life. It couldn't happen soon enough.

"So explain to me again why it took you close to thirty-six hours to call me back when last week you told me to call anytime, anyplace if I found out something important about my mother's death and Laura's disappearance." Jessie stood in Joshua Richards's temporary office trying to stay civil. It wasn't easy. Even though she'd called half a dozen times over the course of the weekend, Richards hadn't returned a call until late Sunday night. Then he put her off until Monday morning.

Now the FBI agent stood behind the glass desk that had nothing on it but a laptop computer, a small notebook and a phone. He looked calmer than Jessie felt he had a right to be. His trim gray suit and white shirt made him look professional and unruffled. Jessie couldn't help but contrast his appearance with Steve, who didn't dress as sharply, but whose dark eyes held compassion.

"I wasn't trying to ignore you, Ms. Barker. I was working another angle of the case. An angle that might bring us close to finding your sister." He was so smooth it felt condescending. Jessica wanted to try and shake him up just a little.

"How about my brother?" If she expected Richards to react to that, she was disappointed. The most she got was the lift of one eyebrow.

"Very good. And you found out about that how?"

"Looking at pictures Steve Gardner and I found this weekend researching the case on the Internet. I know that I have a brother now. And as much as I hoped my mother was not involved with the Brandino family, it's obvious that she was. And it's quite clear there's a lot you haven't bothered to tell me."

Richards only looked slightly more annoyed than before. He slid one finger into the starched collar of his white shirt, loosening the tie that matched the pale blue of his eyes. "Look, if we're going to go into all of this, I'm going to have to insist you sit down. I can have someone bring us coffee…."

Jessie sat in one of two modern, uncomfortable wood-and-metal chairs on the visitors' side of the desk while Joshua slid into the leather executive chair on his side. "I'll sit down briefly but I don't want any coffee. What I want is answers."

He spread out his hands, palms up. "I'll tell you what I can, but I can only go so far. This is still an ongoing investigation, and one I'm ready to take over from the local agencies because of what we've found out so far."

"Do you think Laura is still alive?" She tried not to choke on the words.

For a moment Richards's eyes showed a flash of something that could be compassion…or pity. The first would have surprised her, while the second repelled her. "We have no reason to believe she isn't. That's all I can say for sure right now."

"I know enough about police procedure to know that you couldn't just take over the investigation unless there was a good reason, like a live victim being taken across state lines. As in Laura being taken from Missouri to Michigan."

"That's a possibility. But let me also remind you that I'm part of an organized crime task force. With as much proof as we already have that this involves at least one group like the Brandinos there's enough reason for the task force to be in charge."

The man infuriated her with his measured, careful responses. "How much proof of involvement do you have, other than the fact that my mother is Paula Brandino?" Watching the agent, Jessie thought his look was as evasive as the ones she'd seen from Steve on Saturday. "You have more, even if you can't tell me everything."

"Some of it is just conjecture at this point. Until we have the motive behind your mother's movements and your brother's we can't know for sure why the Brandino family would want to abduct your sister. Kyra says she's got some ideas that might prove helpful but to be honest I don't always understand her explanations. My background's in law enforcement, not medicine."

"Okay, if you were trying to lose me you did so, and normally I'm hard to lose." The smile Richards gave her was brief, but friendly enough that for a moment Jessie understood why Steve didn't trust him. The FBI agent seemed to switch gears when it suited his needs from evasive to engaging. She found herself wishing she'd argued with Steve when he said he wouldn't go along to Richards's office.

"Which part was difficult for you to understand? Personally I get hung up when Kyra or anybody else starts talking about complex issues of genetics."

Jessie shook her head. "That wasn't it at all. I just don't know what my brother's movements back in Detroit might have to do with whatever happened here in St. Charles."

Richards typed something on the keyboard of his computer and looked as if he was waiting for a screen to load. Satisfied he gave a couple of mouse clicks and then turned the machine around so that Jessie could see what he'd done. Before he even started speaking she felt a cold sweat break out at her temples as understanding took root.

Two pictures filled the screen, each of a young man. On the left was the grainy shot she'd seen Saturday of the figure in the front seat of a car. The broad shoulders and dark hair made her think briefly of her father, or at least what she remembered him looking like from her childhood memories.

On the right side of the screen was another photo almost as vague as the first. "This was taken in a grocery store in this county about two months ago as part of their routine surveillance of the customer service desk. The man pictured was cashing a money order."

He was young, with shoulders to match the figure on the left. But this man had black hair instead of the glossy deep brown in the other picture, and it was much longer, caught up at the back of his head. A black T-shirt advertising some sort of martial arts studio replaced the dark sports coat in the first picture.

"The man on the left is Matteo Brandino. We know that for a fact." Richards typed while he talked, and as he did the two photos changed perspective and size and by some computer magic the backgrounds faded while the figures lined up one over the other. Jessie's palms grew damp and her heart beat faster.

"Who is the man on the right?" she asked, trying

to moisten her dry lips. "If you ignore the differences in clothing and hair color, his facial structure lines up with Matteo's."

"That's because we're pretty sure he is Matteo. But for over a month he lived here in St. Charles County. And he went by the name Adrian Bando."

Half a dozen questions crowded Jessie's mind as she tried to process that information. "So he must have gotten in touch with Laura on purpose. She never told me how she found him as a Web site designer. Do you think he was stalking her in some way?"

"Stalking isn't exactly the word I would use. It sounds too menacing, and we don't really think that Matteo particularly meant you or Laura harm. I'd call what he was doing tracking, probably." Joshua pulled his computer back in front of him for a minute and pulled up another screen picture.

"Once Detective Gardner gave us a copy of that picture found near your mother's body we turned it over to one of our computer experts. She found a match on a Web site that lets people search for lost family members or friends."

Sure enough, the photo of Laura and Jessie at their picnic appeared on screen, with a paragraph describing what the searcher knew. It wasn't much; the year the picture was taken and the place, with conjecture as to where the little girls might be now.

"Who do you think did that, my mother or Matteo? And do you have any idea why?"

"Matteo did the technical work for sure. Nothing we've found out about your mother's background once she went back to the family business says she knew anything about computers other than spreadsheets and accounting programs."

Jessie held on to the front of the desk while she willed her hands not to tremble and tried to keep control of her voice. "You still haven't told me what you know about the motive for all this. Do you think that after nearly twenty-five years our mother had some remorse about leaving us by the side of the road?"

"I wish I could tell you. It would make my job easier if we knew the motive behind this. But so far there's only guesses."

"And you're not going to tell me about that." Jessie didn't even bother to frame her statement into a question because she knew what the answer would be. Anger and frustration welled up with the unshed tears stinging her eyes. "How much of this did Detective Gardner know, and how long has he known it?"

Richards's right shoulder lifted in a shrug. "I haven't told him anything, but he's pretty astute. I'd guess he figured out most of this by Friday at the latest. If he has any theories on the motive for your mother's death and your brother and sister's abductions tell him to come in and we'll talk. To tell the truth I was a little surprised to see you alone this morning."

"He's not working this case in a vacuum," Jessie said, aware of how defensive she sounded. It was an issue she wanted to take up with Steve as soon as possible, but in front of Richards she felt the need to be on Steve's side.

"He didn't tell you any of this or you wouldn't have been in my office this early looking as upset as you did when you walked in."

Jessie tried not to wince at the agent's cold and accurate assessment. "You haven't shared much, either. I assume that I'll get a copy of your results when Kyra's done with her report." She pushed herself up from the chair and got ready to leave.

"You will. I'm expecting it tomorrow or Wednesday at the latest, possibly even hand-delivered. What's the best way to contact you?"

Jessie gave him the information and they parted in a civil manner. The lack of time to call Steve or stop by the sheriff's department with this information made her want to kick one of the bare oaks on the way from the building to her parked car. She didn't, mostly because she knew how much it would hurt in her leather flats.

She dialed Gardner's number as she walked, ready to leave him a terse message asking him to set up a meeting later. Instead he answered after the second ring. "Gardner. Major crimes."

"And you've got a major problem, as well, Stephen. I just got out of Joshua Richards's office and we need to talk. But I also have two classes to teach today and that includes giving a pop quiz in less than two hours. How do you want to do this?"

She could hear his sigh over the phone. "It won't help to say I don't want to do it at all, so let's set a time at your favorite coffeehouse."

"Fine. I'm done with class at three. Will that suit you, Detective?"

"As much as anything else. See you then." With that Jessie found herself listening to dead air, wondering how it was possible that she and Steve were this far apart again so very quickly.

ELEVEN

On a Monday afternoon the coffeehouse felt more like a lively college hangout. This time Jessie got there after Steve and she carried her mocha to the booth where he looked way too smug for his own good. "Hi, Jessie. Now before you start in on me, listen to what I have to tell you. I've been doing a little background work today that might make you forgive me for not telling you about Adrian's connection to the family."

"I'm not sure how that's possible, but I think one of the few Bible verses I know is something about turning the other cheek and you'll expect me to do that, so tell me what you know."

She wasn't prepared for the frown her remark caused. "Hey, don't project my faith onto what you're supposed to do, especially if you don't get it right. For now let's put that issue aside and look at what I've found out about Adrian, or Matteo. We probably ought to decide to call him one or the other."

"I think I'd prefer Adrian. Even if it's the name he was hiding behind, I'd rather think of him as something other than a Brandino."

"Makes sense to me. If he got this far away from the family and managed to stay hidden from them for a while, he might want to think of himself as something else, too. Does that make you any more hopeful about your brother?"

Jessie stared down into her cup, wondering what she expected to find there. "I'm so confused. So much has changed since Laura went missing. First I have to deal with my mother turning up, but in such a way that I'll never get to ask her any of the questions I've had since I was six. Now I find out that I have a brother I've never met. Is there any cause for me to feel hopeful about him or not?"

Steve took a piece of paper out of a battered leather portfolio and pushed it across the table toward her. "I think you ought to at least give him the benefit of the doubt. I still don't know why Adrian wanted to find you so much, but he did. He really does seem to be the computer expert he told Laura he was."

"Richards told me about our picture on the missing persons Web site if that's what you mean."

"That's only part of it. Now I'm not the computer expert your brother is, but I know how to use the basics."

Jessie studied the sketch before her. It looked like one of those police artists' renderings, of a young man with long dark hair, a high forehead and a slight cleft in his firm chin. "Did you do this? It's Adrian, isn't it? I recognize the face from the blurry still Agent Richards showed me earlier."

"I plugged the right information into the computer software. These days about half our drawings are done by choosing facial features from options on a program and then blending them together. This was fairly easy because I had that same photo."

"That's where I start to have issues with you, Stephen. You knew all of this Saturday, didn't you?"

He shook his head slowly. "Not really. I suspected that Bando and Brandino might be the same person but I wasn't about to share an idea that would only upset you until I had some proof. Because I knew that if I was right, I'd be telling you about a brother you didn't know existed. You've already had enough pain over all of this without me adding to it if I didn't have to."

"And you wanted to be sure." Jessie could see his point. Even if they were nothing more than casual friends tied together by the hunt for her sister, Steve's police background wouldn't let him upset her without good reason. "But why did you let me go see Richards alone when you had to suspect what he'd tell me?"

"For the reasons I gave you on Saturday. I didn't want to muddy the waters where he's concerned by having him see a personal relationship between us. I'm usually pretty good about hiding my feelings around people, but I knew that if you reacted poorly to finding out about Adrian, I…"

He trailed off and Jessie looked over her glasses at him, trying to urge him to finish his sentence. "You what?"

"I wouldn't be able to disguise my concern. Having Richards and his task force take over the hunt for your sister would be a good thing. They've got a lot more resources than the sheriff's department does. But I don't want him involved just because he thinks I slipped up."

Jessie felt like making a comment about male pride, but then she remembered that Steve hadn't told her what kind of background work he'd been doing today. "We both know you haven't slipped up, Stephen. Now tell me why you looked so pleased with yourself a few minutes ago. It wasn't just for producing this sketch."

"You're right. I've been showing it around a few places. Did you know where Laura liked to take her breaks from work?"

"Sure. Aunt Charlotte's Tearoom about half a block from the salon she worked in, and once in a while when our schedules meshed we even met here."

Steve smiled again. "And the most observant people on the day shift behind the counter both here and at the tearoom recognized this as a man they'd seen with her in the week or so before she disappeared."

"So he'd been trying to make contact with her? Why not with me?" She felt a little left out even though the attention from Adrian had gotten her sister in serious trouble. Jessie felt a pang of guilt knowing that she could have been the one kidnapped instead of her sister but instead he'd chosen Laura. She wished it had been the other way around.

"I wondered that, too. I'd say Adrian knew how to best approach the two of you. He'd been searching for you using computers and missing persons Web sites, and he figured out that Laura was the one most likely to be interested in his services as a Web site designer."

"He had that right. Agent Richards showed me the Web page Adrian made up with our photo. Do you think he was as surprised to find out about us as I was to find about him?" How different would this whole situation be if Jessie had agreed with Laura that they both needed to advertise something online? Looking across the table at Steve again, she could tell he wasn't through. "Okay, what else do you have to show me?"

"You don't give up. I feel like I should take you along next time I have to talk to somebody who's hard to deal with. You're reading me like a book." He sounded more surprised than upset, leading Jessie to think that she had been complimented in an odd sort of way.

Reaching into the portfolio again, Steve put another sketch on the table. "Using what we already knew, and another still from the videos taken from the Brandino compound I was able to put together a decent composite of your mother."

Jessie looked at it. "It shows a lot more detail than what we saw online." The woman was quite attractive, especially for someone middle-aged. Contrasting this picture with Linda Turner seemed to indicate that this woman had led a far more pampered life. "She looks a lot like Laura might in twenty years."

"I'll take your word on that. Personally I think that in the photos I've seen your sister has a more open look and kinder eyes." Steve was blushing again for a moment. "Anyway, when I showed it to

Adrian's neighbors one of them recognized her. She said that the sketch looked like a woman who showed up on Adrian's doorstep two days before the fire and waited for him to get home."

"Do you think that means that she and Laura actually met…maybe got to talk to each other?"

"I'm not sure. I guess we'll have to keep working on finding Laura so you can ask her." The determination in Steve's face made Jessie lose whatever shreds of resentment she'd been holding on to for his reticence earlier. This was a man she could get used to having around. The thought surprised her more than anything else had today, which on a day like this one was saying a lot.

Sometimes Steve thought that he lost all his common sense around Jessie Barker. What crazy notion had made him invite her to a wedding? He should have gone alone and had a nice, quiet afternoon and evening watching his friends tie the knot. Instead here he was all slicked up in a dark suit and tie with Jessie standing next to him giving off a heady scent of perfume that made him think of his mother's flower garden in May. It was nice to see her dressed up in a different way, too. The only other time he'd seen her in anything but business casual had been the navy suit she'd worn to her mother's funeral. Tonight the dress she wore, patterned in warm autumn colors did a lot more to enhance her attractive features.

Rachel made a beautiful bride. Even a hardened old bachelor like him could see how happy she looked, holding hands with Tom and looking into his eyes. He watched them, marveling at Tom's rapt expression. How did it feel to do that, to be in a church full of people and only hear and see one? He stole a glance at Jessie and was surprised to see tears running down her cheeks.

Fishing around in his jacket pocket he found the clean handkerchief he'd put there and handed it to her. "What's up?" She just didn't strike him as the type to cry at weddings.

"I don't usually do this," she said in a whisper so low he could barely hear it. "Laura's the one who cries at weddings. I thought of that and I miss her so much…."

The minister invited everyone to sit down for the exchange of vows. Once they got settled Steve reached over the back of the wooden pew and put his hand on Jessie's shoulder. She'd had a rough week again, which he figured contributed to the tears tonight. After Monday's revelations about her family, things stalled a bit and they knew little more than they had five days before. Richards assured them that there was a constant watch on the Brandino compound but so far it yielded no sign of Adrian or Laura. And he hadn't given Jessie the information he'd apparently promised her on Monday, either.

The most surprising request had been for Jessie to come in to a clinic specified by Richards and have a blood sample drawn. Other than hearing it was for an idea Kyra had from the detailed examination of Dawn, Jessie hadn't gotten a lot of explanation but she went willingly. Steve still felt badly about not being able to go with her, but she'd turned down his offer, saying she wanted to go alone.

"If you change your mind…" he'd offered, but she broke in telling him that if that happened she had the support of a new friend at work. He should probably be glad that the department secretary decided to take Jessie under her wing, but something about the friendship made him a little uncomfortable. Was that warranted or just a bit of jealousy that someone else was comforting her? He'd hoped to introduce Jessie to his mom by now and let her form a friendship there. A tiny sniffle from Jessie drew him back to the present. At the front of the church Tom's brother handed the groom a ring.

"This all looks and sounds a little different to me," Jessie told him. "I never paid much attention to the church part of a church wedding before. Once we get to the reception I'm going to have some questions for you."

"Feel free," Steve told her, ignoring the vibration of his cell phone from the same pocket he'd taken the handkerchief from. Nothing ranked important enough for him to look at that call during a wedding, especially not with Rachel at the altar and Jessie right next to him. If either of the women saw him answering a call now they'd wring his neck.

The wedding looked and sounded different to him, too, but he probably wasn't going to admit that to Jessie. Not when he was seeing it through a new lens because of her. Had he ever tried to imagine himself up there getting married before? Even now it was a vague image because of all the barriers between them. At least the FBI had taken over enough of the investigation that he didn't feel out of line taking her to an event like this one.

But her life was on hold right now and he had no idea what part he'd play in it once things resolved. The longer the case dragged on the harder it was to believe they'd find Laura alive and well. He'd tried to entrust that problem entirely to God but it wasn't easy. It would be a foreign concept to Jessie: how he could take one of the heaviest problems in his life and turn over the worry like that.

Therein lay the rest of his hesitation. For him, faith was an everyday part of life; for Jessie that was a new concept. Until their beliefs came a little closer to matching he couldn't really consider marriage. While he didn't share the fervor of some Christians to avoid being "unequally yoked" to a nonbeliever he'd always taken for granted that if he ever married it would be to a godly woman.

The minister introduced Tom and Rachel for the first time as a married couple and the applause through the church made Steve smile. He couldn't get too discouraged about his situation while watching the couple in the front of the church. If God could bring Rachel together with the right man through a bad softball play, surely the obstacles between Jessie and him weren't insurmountable, either.

Jessie perked up a little by the time they left the church. "So, on to the reception?"

He fished the cell phone out of his pocket. "In just a minute. I need to see who called me during the wedding. I wasn't about to look then."

"Good idea. No matter how good a friend Rachel is, I don't think she would have wanted that distraction during her wedding."

The number didn't mean much, but there was a message and he listened to it. Joshua Richards identified himself and told him he was looking for Jessie. They'd settled into Steve's car by then and he looked over at her in the passenger seat. "You have any idea why Joshua Richards would be looking for you this time of evening on a Saturday?"

She frowned slightly. "Checking up on me, I guess. Maybe I should have taken what he said Thursday more seriously."

Okay, now she had his interest. "And what did he say that you decided to ignore?"

She waved a hand at him. "That makes it sound a lot more serious. Once I went to the clinic for my blood tests he told me he wanted me to keep a low profile for a little while."

"How low a profile are we talking?" Steve asked, neck and shoulder muscles starting to tense.

"I'm not under house arrest or anything. He said that I could go to work and other necessary trips, but otherwise he wanted my cooperation in keeping my life quiet."

"Maybe I should be flattered you think going to a wedding with me is a necessary trip, but I expect Agent Richards might think differently."

She looked away, like a guilty kid. "Maybe so. Does this mean you're going to take me home?"

"Not yet. Let me call Richards first and see what he has to say." He thought for a minute. "I'm going to step outside the car to talk to him, and while I do that I'm going to lock you in."

"Isn't that a little much?"

"Not until I find out why that FBI agent is looking for you. If you're in danger I'm not going to be the person that fails to protect you. And knowing your stubbornness, Jessie, this is the one way I can think of to keep you right here." She made a face, but she didn't argue and Steve called the FBI man. "Jessie's with me. We've been at a wedding. Something happened?"

"Not really. We're getting close and I don't like what we've found so far. There's more going on than just the Brandino family involvement. Make sure you keep very close track of that woman, since she won't listen to me, and be careful."

"I won't let her out of my sight." They signed off and Steve looked through the window at the lovely woman in his car. It was nice to have an excuse to be close to Jessie all evening. Steve could hardly wait to get back in the car and tell her they were together for the rest of the night.

TWELVE

"So, is this a date or are you my bodyguard now?" Jessie didn't know why she felt so prickly about the situation when so little had changed. Half an hour before, she wanted to stay out with Steve as long as possible. But once he came back to the car and told her Richards said not to let her out of his sight, it didn't exactly feel like the same pleasant evening.

Steve didn't seem nearly as unhappy about things as she felt. But then, he was here at his friend's wedding reception enjoying the buzz of people around them. Jessie felt a little out of place because other than the bride and groom, she didn't know anybody here except Steve.

"I guess we better call it a date, because I'm not allowed to moonlight doing private security work." Steve's smile was almost flirtatious. "Besides, I don't think bodyguards usually pay much attention to comfort, just keeping somebody alive. So as your date, I'm ready to get us both into that buffet line and have something to eat. How about you?"

"Now that you mention it, I am fairly hungry. And that punch bowl we walked past when we came in looked tempting, too."

"Then let's go take care of all that and come back to meet our tablemates. I know it might be a little odd for you, since you don't recognize most of these people. To tell the truth I don't know a lot of them, either."

"Okay, that surprises me. I figured you'd know everybody. I feel a little better knowing I'm not the only one." Jessie got up and headed toward the buffet table, Steve following closely.

"I recognize people from church, but Rachel and Tom must have pretty big families, and folks they work with are here, too. But that's all right. I'm happy with the people I do know." Jessie felt his hand, warm and protective on her back. His words and his touch put her at ease.

"Back there during the ceremony you said you had questions for me. What were they?" Steve asked as they balanced plates and punch cups on their way back to the table.

Jessie wasn't sure what to ask first. "Wow. It's hard to know where to start. Was that a fairly typical wedding ceremony, or was it different because Tom's a minister?"

Gardner's brow furrowed for a minute before he answered. "I think it was pretty normal, judging from the ones I've seen. Why?"

Jessie felt herself blushing. "It all seemed so serious, and so intense. There wasn't a lot of difference in the promises they made to each other but they had a different gravity because of how much they brought God into the relationship."

"For a believer, that's the way it's got to be. Without God as the most important part of a marriage, there's not much left to fall back on when things get rough. If we're not trying to discern and follow God's plan for our lives, then making marriage work would be a constant struggle."

"Isn't it anyway?" Jessie blurted out.

Steve gave her an intense look. "I don't know if I'd call it a struggle exactly, from what I've seen. Maybe more of a challenge. Struggle sounds so negative. Of course I'm just speaking from outside the picture here, since I've never been married."

"Me, neither." They put their plates and cups on the table and sat down. "I have to admit that for people saying such serious things, Rachel and Tom looked incredibly happy."

Steve smiled. "They did, didn't they? And if you

look around the room and find them you'll see those grins are still on their faces. That's because those promises they made bound them together and set them free at the same time."

"All right, that's heavier than I can understand right now. And your food's going to get cold if you spend much time explaining it. Isn't there any simple way to explain this?"

"I guess. Do you have a Bible at home?"

Jessie groaned inwardly. "Probably. I don't know how much of it I'd understand if I read it, though."

"Just start out easy. Read the first few chapters of Genesis, the first book of the Old Testament. It's enough to read those and see what God thinks of each one of us, and how much God values us. And right there in that first part of the story God says it isn't good for man to be alone, that he needs company."

The way Steve looked at her while he was telling her that made Jessie feel different from any other time in her life. She felt special and valued and she wondered if it was some spark of God coming through Steve's dark eyes and the warmth of his hand on top of hers. Love just glowed through him and it nearly brought her to tears. Was she seeing Steve's love of God, or another kind of love altogether? Her mouth felt dry and she needed some of that punch.

Before they could go any further in their discussion three more people planted themselves at the table, chatting and visiting and introducing themselves. Steve gave her a wink and a shrug that made her heart flutter a little.

Anticipating that time alone made the wedding reception seem hours longer than it was. Steve had been right about Rachel and Tom; wherever she saw them together or alone that evening they were smiling. The smiles seemed the broadest when they visited the different tables together, Tom's white-shirted arm around the frothy lace on Rachel's shoulders. For the first time in her adult life Jessie allowed herself to actually consider how nice it might be if she were in a similar position.

She probably needed her head examined, but now that she'd met Stephen and gotten to know him she could imagine being married. Before knowing him she hadn't even given a lifetime commitment to someone an idle thought. Jessie had been alone and responsible for herself, and for Laura, for so long that the notion of having someone in her life to care about her and for her was totally foreign. Now, watching Tom and Rachel, she saw what a real loving relationship could look like and she liked what she saw.

"Hey, Jessie. You still in there? I think they're

going to cut the cake if you want some." She snapped back to the present with Steve's voice and wondered what he must think of her sitting there with a goofy smile on her face.

Cake sounded good. "They won't do that awful thing where they push cake into each other's faces, will they? Because if they do, I'm out of here."

Steve shook his head. "Don't worry. I think Rachel would be out of here, too, if anybody tried that, and Tom has too much respect for her to consider it. I'm glad to hear you don't like that nonsense either. I've always thought it was juvenile and distasteful, but I'm the minority opinion."

"Well, we can be the minority opinion together," Jessie told him, welcoming the chance to have his arm linked with hers as they got up and crossed the large room to watch along with the other guests as the bride and groom cut the cake.

When she tried to hide a yawn about forty-five minutes later, Steve started gathering up his suit coat and making goodbyes. "I promised I'd get Jessie home safe, sound and early," he told the rest of the table. Her eyes felt heavy enough she wasn't about to argue. It had been a nice evening but going home sounded good. Besides, she'd left Maude alone for quite a few hours and she wasn't sure what would greet her on her return.

Steve helped her into her coat and they found his car in the crowded lot. Puffs of steam rose around them as they breathed in the cold air. "I know it's supposed to be fall for another month, but nights are beginning to feel like winter is on the way," Jessie said, wishing she'd remembered to stick gloves in her coat pockets.

Steve took her hand, sharing the warmth of his own. "I don't have gloves, either, but this will help a bit."

"I didn't think I was that obvious," Jessie told him, almost wishing it were farther to the car so she could keep holding his hand.

"You probably wouldn't be to most people, but we've been hanging around each other a lot lately."

"Too much?" Jessie asked, afraid of the answer once the words were out of her mouth.

Steve was silent for a few moments, making her even a little more nervous. He opened her car door and made sure she was in comfortably and went around to the driver's side. "No, I wouldn't say too much. It could be under better circumstances. With all that's happened since we've known each other, do you think there's a chance that you could be around me without thinking of all the bad things you've experienced in the last month?"

Steve's expression looked the way Jessie thought

she must look. Wary, hopeful and yet unsure of whether he wanted her to answer. She also understood why it had taken him a little while to answer her equally prickly question. While he waited he started the car, turned on the heater and drove out of the parking lot. When the radio got a little louder he clicked it off. "I think I'd like to keep seeing you, Steve. But we need to get through the next few days or weeks, whatever it takes to find Laura."

"Okay." Steve didn't turn the radio back on or play a CD, but the unspoken words hung between them in the car. For the first time neither of them had jumped to say anything right away about how Laura might be found. In her research on urban legends Jessie knew that there was truth to the saying that the first forty-eight hours were key in a murder investigation or a kidnapping. She found herself hoping that in Laura's case things would still work in their favor even though so much time had elapsed.

Steve's good driving and the lateness of the hour must have lulled her to sleep. The next thing Jessie knew Steve was gently shaking her shoulder and calling her name. "Hey, we're at your house. I think I better walk you in, don't you?"

Jessie tried to clear the cobwebs from her tired brain and protest that she could get in all by herself but she lost the battle. "That might be nice," she said. Steve came around to the passenger side of the car while she gathered her purse and found her keys.

She expected to hear barking the minute she turned the key in the lock. "I put Maude in the kitchen before we left so she didn't have the run of the whole condo. I don't want to put too much temptation in her way until I'm sure she's as well behaved as she seems."

The door opened, but there was still no sound from Maude. "That's kind of odd. Every other time I've come in the front door she's barked like crazy. Do you think she's that sound asleep?"

"I doubt it. Let me come in with you and see what's going on. Don't go too far without me," Steve warned.

The cool air had woken Jessie up and she thought he was being much too protective. Just then she heard whining and scratching. "I know what happened. She somehow got into the laundry room and shut the door on herself. Poor baby," she said, hurrying to the kitchen to set her unhappy dog free.

"Jessie, I said wait," Steve said, his voice more intense now. But she was to the kitchen and over the dog-gate before he could figure out the latch and follow her. Opening the laundry room door she started talking to Maude to calm her down but before she could get out more than a word something slammed her across the hallway into a wall and she let out a yelp. The air knocked out of her, she couldn't make any more sound. In the midst of the commotion Steve, trying to vault the gate, got a foot caught in it and he and the gate came crashing to the floor.

Jessie found her voice at the same time whoever had pushed her against the wall took rough hold of her left arm and shoulder and started pulling her into the garage. For a moment she thought she felt cold metal along the side of her face and she cried out, pulling away as much as she could. In that moment Steve burst through the doorway from the condo and yelled, "Police. Let go of her and freeze." Instead the masked figure pushed Jessie hard into her car, setting off the motion alarm and in the confusion that followed, sprinted out the door. Steve was there instantly picking her up off the concrete floor of the garage where she'd landed. "Are you okay?"

"Nothing broken," Jessie managed. "Don't worry over me. He's getting away." Her attacker must have been in very good shape, because by the time Steve steadied her against the still-wailing car and went out to give chase, they could hear a car door slam and an engine start in rapid succession. Jessie ran to the doorway. "It sounds like it's on the cul-de-sac behind us." Wincing, she could feel a spot where her knee had scraped something metal and a small trickle of blood ran down her leg.

She switched on the light and went back to the kitchen as quickly as she could to find her car keys. Finally the alarm stopped its racket and Steve came back into the garage. "I didn't even get a plate number," he complained, sounding winded. "Are you sure you're okay? Because I'm going to get you inside under bright lights and if I have any doubts we're calling for an ambulance along with the sheriff's department."

"I think I'll be all right." Already she could feel different spots on her body that would be sore and bruised tomorrow, but nothing seemed to be broken and she hadn't ever hit her head.

Steve eased her into one of the kitchen chairs. Once she sat down Jessie realized that now Maude was barking. She tried to get up to go and open the door to the powder room near the laundry but Steve put a hand on her shoulder. "Stay there and I'll get her." Once the door opened Maude sprang out barking, dashing between Jessie and Steve in a frantic arc. Steve used the kitchen phone to call the sheriff's department, apparently getting hold of a dispatcher, giving them as much detail as he could. Once done with his call he got down on one knee on the kitchen floor and called Maude.

"No signs that anybody tried to hurt her," he said. "You both got lucky on that score. He must have wanted to use her as bait to draw you into the house quickly."

Jessie shivered. "I'm glad she's okay. And I'm pretty sure that I will be, too, with a little first aid." Lifting the hem of her dress she looked at her knee. There were a few small bits of debris ground into her skin, but not enough of a cut to need stitches. Now that the worst was over she felt shaky and exhausted.

Steve had come over to examine her knee. She winced when he touched it. "Sorry. I don't want to hurt you but we should clean this out and put a bandage on it at least. Tell me where you keep the first aid supplies and I'll go get them."

Jessie didn't feel like arguing so she directed him to the shelf in the linen closet upstairs where he could find the right things. While he did that she went into the powder room and removed her shredded panty hose. When Steve came back she insisted on using the disinfectant wipes by herself, unwilling to let him cause her pain. "Once I'm done you can help with the antibiotic cream and bandages. Maybe by then someone from your department will be here."

Her prediction was right. While Steve pointed out things to the deputy with a camera Jessie got permission to go upstairs and change into soft velour sweats and take a couple of antiinflammatory tablets. He insisted the female deputy go with her to check the walk-in closet and bathroom, and stay close in case she felt faint.

Going downstairs again Jessie just knew it must be midnight at least. Giving her statement to the officers felt like an ordeal and she breathed a sigh of relief once they'd finished. By then she felt rooted to the couch, Maude curled up beside her, refusing to leave her side. Steve sat on the love seat, a line of concern tracing the middle of his brow. "Agent Richards didn't think much of my protecting you tonight. In fact he's ready to come over and take you to a safe house immediately."

"I won't go. I know I can't stay here alone tonight, but I'm not going to an official safe house." The idea made her shudder.

"That's what I told him you'd say. And since he doesn't have the power to force you to do anything, we made a compromise. As long as I take you somewhere you'll be safe and no one's likely to find you, he's all right with that."

"Good. And whatever you come up with, it better include plans for Maude because I'm not leaving her here, either." Jessie knew she sounded like a petulant child but tonight she and the dog were a package deal.

"I figured on that, too. I've already made a phone call to the place I want to take you, and it's okay with the owner if you bring your dog. Let's go upstairs and I'll help you pack what you need for a day or two, all right?"

Jessie nodded, having spent all her energy on resisting the safe house idea. This sounded like as good a compromise as she would get. "Stephen, as long as you and Maude both stick around tonight, I'm good. So where are we going?"

Steve gave a wry smile and ushered her up the stairs. "I'd really hoped to take you home to meet my mom sometime soon, just not this soon. I think you'll like it there. The security's good, she cooks better than Miss Ella and there's plenty of room for all of us."

He was kidding, right? Jessie assured herself that he was just talking about taking her home to distract her from whatever he really had planned. An hour later Jessie found out that Steve hadn't been joking about any of it. In short order she and Maude were sleeping in a room still decorated with twenty-year-old rock band posters and several basketball trophies. She resolved to find out everything she could from Steve's mom about the man, but it would have to wait until daylight.

THIRTEEN

Jessie woke up to sunlight, the sound of soft music somewhere in the house and the smell of bacon. The door to the bedroom was open slightly and she was alone in the room. That didn't totally disturb her, because if she could smell breakfast up here on the second floor, she knew Maude had probably sniffed it out long before.

She grabbed her toiletries and made herself a little more presentable in the hall bathroom. Her knee reminded her of everything that had gone on the night before, especially when she went down the stairs to find the kitchen.

"Great, you're up," Susan Gardner said over her shoulder as she stood at the stove. "Your dog is a real sweetie. I hope it was all right that I scrambled an egg and gave it to her."

Maude sat in a corner with a bright flowered

china bowl in front of her. Her trademark smile was even broader than usual. "All right? I think you've got a friend for life," Jessie said, laughing.

"Good. Some of my best friends have four legs. If you ever need somebody to watch her, let me know. Now how are you feeling this morning? Stephen hasn't said much about what's going on with you, but it must be serious or he wouldn't have brought you here."

"I'm…all right. My leg's sore where I knocked into a car and then landed on the garage floor. Things would have been a lot worse if Steve hadn't been there. But then I'm sure you've heard that before."

"Too often. I'm proud of him and worried about him at the same time when somebody says that." Looking at her closely, Jessie could see that Steve had his mother's eyes. Otherwise he must have taken after his father's side of the family because Susan was a small, compact woman whose mostly silver hair was a mop of curls. "I've already made a pot of coffee. When my son's home it's just automatic to brew that much. When it's only me I make about two cups. Can I pour you some?"

"I'll get it myself if you'll just tell me where the mugs are. You shouldn't have to wait on me."

Finding the mugs let Jessie also find the plates to set the kitchen table with, and looking around the kitchen she was able to figure out which drawer most likely held the silverware, as well. "Okay, if Stephen doesn't choose to keep you around, I might have to adopt you myself," Susan said, her impish smile showing a dimple on one cheek. "He's never brought anybody like you home before."

"I hardly ever bring anybody home, period, Mom. And when I do it's usually somebody from the department who is down on his luck," Steve said from where he lounged in the doorway. He must have been watching the two of them for a little while. He looked as if he'd been outside and he carried a bundle of newspapers under one arm. "Sunday papers. I know you like to do the crossword."

He put the papers on a chair and crossed the kitchen to drop a kiss on the top of his mother's head. Watching the two of them gave Jessie a warm feeling inside. What was it like to have a loving, uncomplicated relationship with a parent? For her it would always remain an unanswered question.

For Stephen it was a given in his life. It made Jessie wonder if having that relationship made it easier for him to accept that God could love him even more than his earthly parents. When you had loving people in your life to begin with, surely it helped with the belief that God was out there somewhere and loved you.

"Okay, you look thoughtful," Steve said, startling her a little when he put an arm around her. "Or are you still just waking up?"

"A little of both. I smelled the bacon and came down to join everybody else. I haven't gotten to ask your mom most of the questions that I wanted to, but I thought that maybe I could find out a few things about you over breakfast."

Steve opened his mouth as if to argue with that, but Susan spoke first. "You ask anything you want, Jessie. I'll be more than happy to tell you all about Stephen. I've been looking forward to this for years."

Steve groaned. "I'm going to regret all the times I missed curfew and brought home detention slips for you to sign from school, huh?"

His mother laughed. "Are you ever." She turned to Jessie. "When we're done eating, remind me to get out my photo albums."

Steve put his hands on Jessie's shoulders. "Please believe me when I say that I passed every part of the police academy course with flying colors and I'm a respected detective and deputy. Things I did when I was fourteen have absolutely no bearing on my competency today."

She stretched up and kissed him on the cheek. "I know that, Stephen. And I still want to hear the stories about your high school escapades. You've heard too much about me because of this investigation. Now I want to hear about you."

Steve laughed. "Fair enough, I guess. And I have to admit I deserve anything Mom dishes out."

"Including scrambled eggs and homemade cinnamon rolls, so sit down while they're still hot," Susan told him as she started serving breakfast.

Two hours later the lightness of the morning gave way to a much more serious afternoon. "You know that Agent Richards won't let us wait until tomorrow to talk about what happened at your place last night. When I was out getting the newspaper earlier he and I talked," Steve told Jessie as she dried the last of the dishes he'd been washing.

"So where do I go now?" She tried not to sound too unhappy. It made sense that the FBI wanted to be part of the investigation. She just hoped it didn't mean that she'd have to go somewhere she'd hate.

"For now, we keep things the way they are and you'll stay here. You can go back to your condo and pick up more things as you need them, but only with somebody from our department or the FBI with you, and never directly from this house."

"Okay. I guess I should be grateful that nobody's pushing the safe house idea. Will you be along when I talk to Agent Richards?"

"I wouldn't miss it. We're meeting at his office and then going over things at your condo. I'm not letting you out of my sight today, Jessie. After last night I want to make sure we can keep you safe."

"It will have to be an effort we all take part in, Stephen. I'm not going to trust my safety to anybody else anymore without getting fully involved." Even as she said the words Jessie felt stronger and more in control.

Steve drove, uncharacteristically silent. Jessie let him alone for a little while, then had to break the quiet. "What's up? I expected an answer from you after I said that."

"There are things I want to say, but I don't think you'll want to hear them. I'd like you to be able to trust your safety to another, but not to me and not to the FBI. I keep hoping that my words and actions will help lead you to put your trust where it belongs, in God. And doing that, especially at first, is the ultimate loss of control because you have to give up all your own power and surrender it to the Lord instead."

Jessie felt like reaching out and touching Steve's cheek, where the tension in his face showed through. "This is a conversation we need to have when we can face each other without distractions. Let's make it soon, all right?"

His expression softened into something like surprise. "All right. Once we're done with Richards maybe we can talk about it." He pulled into the parking garage of the county building where Richards set up his headquarters. On a Sunday afternoon there weren't many cars around. At first Jessie felt unprotected. Then she realized that the empty parking garage meant there would be fewer places for the bad guys to hide.

Steve seemed wary all the way up to Richard's office. And when they got to the office Jessie felt a small shock at seeing Kyra Elliott there. It was a relief to see a familiar face, and one capable of smiling. Joshua, at least, appeared to have lost that ability.

"Special Agent Richards tells me that you had a rough night. I'm glad to see that you're okay," Kyra said. Jessie got the feeling she might have hugged her if the situation had been a little less tense. "Now, I'm not sure how much you're going to like what I have to say…"

Jessie raised a hand, palm toward Kyra. "Don't worry about that. I've found enough things out in the last week that I believe, even without your evidence, that my mom was Paula Brandino. If any good can come out of that, it will be that when this is all over I may gain a brother out of it all."

"That would be good. I've found out a couple of things this week myself and they could make finding him a little bit easier." Kyra smiled slightly. "And even better, they could explain why someone would want to take your sister."

Agent Richards motioned to the round table near the window. "How about we all sit down together and Dr. Elliott can tell us what she's found?"

Jessie thought she saw Kyra's nose wrinkle when Richards referred to her as "Dr. Elliott" but if she did it was over in a flash. Soon there were graphs and printouts on papers all over the table and Kyra was drawing more notes as the rest of them watched. "I'll try not to get too deep into genetics and DNA explanations for all this, but if I slip up, tell me." She looked across the table at Jessie. "Have you ever given blood?"

"Yes. Once a year the community college has a blood drive, and I try to go every year. I talked Laura into it once but she couldn't do it."

"Do you know why?"

Jessie wasn't sure where all of this was leading, but she searched her memory for the answer. "There was something about the way her blood clotted, or didn't, that they didn't like. I remember she asked if she should see a doctor, and the nurse in charge of the drive just told her to be sure to have regular checkups."

Kyra nodded, looking thoughtful. Steve squirmed in his chair. "Why is all of this important? Did you identify Jessie's mother because of some rare blood factor?"

"In a way. Paula Brandino apparently had the genetic markers for a kind of leukemia that can be hereditary. She didn't have the disease herself, but it was always a possibility that she'd pass it on to her children. It seems in the case of your brother that happened."

"Did he know his illness was hereditary?" Steve leaned forward in interest.

Joshua answered his question. "We think he did. And for that matter it looks like Jake Brandino found out, as well. Matteo probably knew that his uncle would go to any lengths he could to keep him healthy."

"Do you think that's why he pulled away from the crime family?" Jessie found herself holding her breath waiting for the answer.

"It's hard to tell because our contacts back to the Brandino organization have paid more attention to Jake than to Matteo up until recently. But yes, there's a chance that's why your brother tried to change his identity. We have reason to believe that before he left, your mother finally told him about you and Laura."

"That would explain the picture we found, and the Web site searching for us." Knowing that Adrian could have been looking for them for a good reason made Jessie's heart flutter. "Isn't the treatment for most kinds of leukemia a bone marrow transplant?"

Kyra spoke up. "That's right. Bone marrow or stem cells from a healthy, compatible donor are the best chance for survival in most cases. And a full sibling is often the best match."

"So they might have snatched Laura to use her as a donor for her brother?" Steve leaned back in his chair. "But how did Paula get involved, and why kill her?"

Joshua scowled. "That's the hardest question to answer. But if we're being truly cynical, Paula may have lost a lot of her value to Jake Brandino once she led him back to her son, and the sister who could make him healthy again."

Jessie felt chilled throughout her body. "So they might have tracked my sister and brother through my mom, and then killed her? How could anyone do that?"

Kyra put a smooth, long-fingered hand on top of hers for support. "It isn't something most normal people would do. Jake doesn't fall under most people's descriptions of normal, though, and he'd do anything to get his second-in-command back and healthy."

"He got him back," Richards said. "And now we just have to figure out where he's trying to make the young man healthy."

"Let's get going on that, and fast," Steve said. Jessie wasn't sure why he was so insistent all of a sudden. She gave him a questioning look.

"I may be working in law enforcement, but I know a little bit about medicine, too. About eighteen months ago a friend in the department had a bone marrow transplant, so I know how the process works. Sometimes even a family donor doesn't work out. If it was Brandino's guys trying to take Jessie, then it must mean that they think they need another donor. If we want to find Laura alive and healthy, it has to be soon."

By midmorning Tuesday Jessie couldn't sit still with Steve in her office. He watched her get up from the desk, pace around the room, take books off the shelf and sit down again, only to do it all again. "Why are you still here? Why aren't all of you in Detroit arresting Brandino and finding Laura?"

"There's nothing to arrest Brandino for right now, Jessie. You have to know how careful guys like that are to keep themselves clean. And the moment

Richards and the FBI move out I'm going with them. Until then my job is to keep an eye on you."

"Well, I don't like being watched. I can't concentrate," she grumbled. "Instead of just sitting there watching me why don't you make yourself useful?"

"How? I'm guessing you don't just want to be distracted."

She gave him the kind of look she probably gave students who tried to talk her into a better grade. "Not exactly. Get on that laptop and help me with research. I have a feeling there's even more to all of this than we already know and if I can't do anything else, I'm going to figure that part out."

"Yes, ma'am." It was good to see Jessie with a purpose. Her blue-gray eyes glinted and she began firing directions at him. In a couple of minutes he had to slow her down. "You're good at this speed research, but I can't quite keep up. This department-issue computer isn't as fast as what you're using and I don't type all that fast."

"You're probably good at law enforcement history. Guide me through a little background on the U.S. Marshals service. Richards said they were responsible for the witness protection program."

"They were, until after 9/11. Now there's a separate agency that oversees the program. But before, it was all theirs."

"If something went wrong inside the agency, would it have been covered up, or could it have made headlines?"

"It could only have been kept quiet to a degree. Why? Do you think somebody in the government had something to do with your mother's disappearance?" The thought had some merit. Even more possible was that Brandino had gotten to someone and made it worth their while. "You were six when the accident happened, right?"

"And Laura was four." Steve did the math, knowing their current ages, and started searching sites related to the federal marshals.

What he found had him shaking his head in disbelief. "Uh, Jessie? You want to come over and look at this?" She came and stood behind him and Steve could feel the pressure of her hands on his shoulders. At first her touch was soft, and then gradually he could feel her fingers start to tremble.

"Where was the office those three worked out of?" Her voice shook almost as much as her fingers.

"Chicago." When Jessie heard that she went back to her desk and Steve watched her pale face while she typed.

"Elgin, Illinois," she read.

"Samuel Myers, age forty, died suddenly at his home. Myers, a federal marshal, was not on duty at the time of his death. He leaves a wife, Deborah and two children, a son Joshua and a daughter…"

And then her voice broke. Jessie covered her face with her hands and Steve was beside her in a heartbeat.

He looked at the picture on the screen of her computer. "Looks like we need to go back and talk to the Special Agent. And this time we'll be the ones asking the questions."

At least the man was truthful. He focused on the opposite wall, as if he was looking through Jessie when he spoke, but he didn't pull any punches.

"When I was ten my father went out to our family garage next to the alley behind our house and shot himself with his service revolver. At least that was what everyone said. The claim was that the marshals service had traced a large, unexplained amount of money to him at the same time several witnesses died or disappeared. But no one ever found the money."

"Does the FBI know all this?" Jessie's voice was harsh.

Richards's head snapped back as if she'd slapped him. "Of course. They also know why my mother insisted that my sister and I take her maiden name, and they know that I've never believed my father was guilty."

"Was anyone else involved?" Steve felt the man's pain, but he still wasn't ready to drop his anger because he hadn't told them all of this to begin with.

"Two other marshals were suspected but they made it through all investigations with no charges at the time."

"What about later?"

"They're both dead. And both under suspicious circumstances. Cassidy's car went into a lake and Patrick's lake cabin burned to the ground with him in it." Richards's voice sounded flat. "And I'm determined that no other family has to go through what my family did because of the Brandino crime family."

Jessie stood straight in front of him and looked him directly in the face. "Then put that determination to work and find my sister."

"I think we have. I'm waiting on reports from an undercover team and helicopter surveillance. Since you know this much, you might as well stay. We're going to be acting on the information as soon as we verify that we've found the private medical clinic where she's being held."

Steve expected Jessie might lose it at that point,

but she didn't. Richards got them settled with coffee in a small room nearby and went back to his office.

"This wasn't the way I expected this to happen," Steve told Jessie as they sat quietly. "It looks like we're finally getting someplace."

"I know. And I'm scared." Jessie's hands wrapped around her mug so that her knuckles were white. "I want to pray about this, Steve. Please, show me how."

Setting aside the coffee mugs, Steve took her hands in his and softly, with their heads almost touching over the table, he started speaking. "Heavenly Father, You hold us all in the palm of Your hand. We know that Laura is there just as we are, and You know where she is. Please guide the men and women who seek for her, and keep her protected until we can find her."

He paused to collect his thoughts and give Jessie a chance to continue. She took a long, deep breath before she said anything. "Lord, I want to know You. I want the peace that Steve has, that I've seen through him and Kyra and others. And please, I want the chance to share that peace with Laura if I can." She stopped then and Steve kept hold of her hands.

"We ask all this in the name of Jesus. Amen." She echoed his amen and leaned into him where they sat in silence more peaceful than any he had ever known.

FOURTEEN

The office suite Joshua Richards had commandeered had a waiting room with a leather sofa and two matching chairs. When hours had gone by and there still hadn't been a final word on the location of the clinic, Steve insisted that Jessie stretch out for a while on the sofa while he brought an office chair into the room. "I don't want to fall asleep while you rest." Jessie, still overwhelmed by the feelings that had swept over her when she prayed earlier, didn't argue for a change, but just went along.

She didn't think she'd really do more than doze. That's why it was a surprise when Joshua's voice woke her out of a sound sleep. "Be thankful we kept searching," he was saying to Steve. "The trail to the Upper Peninsula was a phony, designed to throw us or anybody else looking for them off the scent.

They're in Ontario, about halfway between Windsor and a very small town called Essex."

"That's trouble, isn't it? You don't have any jurisdiction to go in there."

"Yeah, but we've got friends. The task force I'm part of has an equivalent in the RCMP. And they'd like to snag Jake Brandino just as much as I would."

Jessie was sitting straight up now, trying to figure out what the best argument would be for not getting left behind. "You have to take us with you. I've got to be there when you find Laura."

"You have no idea how many strings I had to pull and how many favors I had to call in, but you're both going. Not to be part of the raid on the clinic, but you to positively identify your sister and Steve because I figured you wouldn't go otherwise. You'll be kept in one of our surveillance vehicles."

Jessie sat back, stunned. "What kind of argument did you have to give them to take a Missouri sheriff's department deputy on this raid?"

"He's an identification expert aiding the bureau. And if either of you are injured in the operation we're going to be in a world of trouble so Steve had better be as good as I think he'll be at protecting the two of you."

Steve's face was stony. "Don't worry. I won't let you down. I promised Jessie I'd do anything in my power to find her sister and I'm not backing down now."

"Then go home, pack and be at Spirit of St. Louis Airport at eight tonight. If you don't show up on time, we leave without you."

It only took a look from Steve to get Jessie up and moving. Speeding through the streets of the city in Steve's car she prayed her second heartfelt prayer, this one of thanks for the incredible gift she had received today.

"I still want you to stay here. You know that." Steve stood in the doorway of Jessie's bedroom watching her pack. "You could stay with my mom and go to work, keep up the facade of a normal life in case anybody's watching you. It's not going to be safe where we're going and I'll worry about you the whole time."

Jessie nodded, trying to give him the attention he deserved while concentrating on packing for the next few days. Whether she followed Steve and Joshua or stayed with Susan she would still need to take clothes from the condo because staying here alone wasn't an option. "You're right. I know that you're right. But just like you, I'm not backing down now."

Steve looked heavenward with a sigh. "At least I tried to get you to stay here. And I still wish you would. But short of having you arrested I can't think of a way to keep you here."

"I'm truly touched by your need to protect me. Between you and your mom, I've never felt so cared for in my life." Jessie felt tears well up again. She'd cried more in the last month than in the fifteen years before that, and it was getting to be a tiresome feeling. "But this time I've got to go and do this. If I didn't go and I missed my last chance to see Laura, I'd never forgive myself."

"So what can I do to get us out of here faster?" When he stopped arguing Jessie felt like kissing Steve.

"Go down to the pantry and grab a grocery sack. Put all of Maude's food and toys you can find into it so that your mom isn't inconvenienced any more than she has to be. And grab the dog bed so we can put that in your trunk with the stuff we really need."

Steve gave her the ghost of a smile. "I have an idea that dog bed has never been used. And knowing my mom, it's not likely to be used there, either. Maude is going to get the same kind of spoiling at her house that she'd get here."

Jessie smiled back and kept packing. Once she had the essentials for herself in the small suitcase, she zipped it up and brought it to the other bedroom. There she found Laura's favorite pink velour pants and hoodie and a T-shirt with Princess written across the front in glittery letters. "Now I'm packing this because I'm trying my hardest to trust that we're going to find her and she's going to be in good enough shape to want her own clothes," she said softly. It still felt a little funny to talk to God, but it got more natural every time she tried it.

"What about this box of treats?" Steve called up the stairs.

"Sure, why not?" Jessie zipped the suitcase a final time and hurried down to meet him. If her adrenaline was pumping this fast and they still had a couple of hours to go before they left St. Louis, what would it be like in Canada?

Having her cell phone ring in her purse made her heart race even faster. She hoped it wasn't Richards calling to tell her he'd changed his mind. Looking at the display she felt relief when she saw the familiar number at the history office.

"Professor Barker? It's Linda. I'm getting ready to go home soon and I noticed that your lights are still on, your office unlocked and your computer running on the desk. Do you want me to take care of that for you?"

"That would be great," Jessie said. Then she came to a dead stop in the front hall. Her passport was at work in her desk! "Actually, you don't have to do all of that. Just turn off the computer and close it and turn the office lights out. Leave the door unlocked because I just realized I have to come in for a minute or two. I'll pick up the computer and the other things I need and lock up."

"If you say so. I could bring your computer to you if you're at home," Linda offered.

"That's very kind of you, but I need to get something out of the locked drawer of my desk, so I have to be there anyway."

"All right, then. I guess I'll see you in the morning."

"Actually, I'm going to have to take a few days' emergency leave. But I'll work that out with the department head and let you know when I come back."

They said quick goodbyes and Jessie took her suitcase out to the car so that she could break the news to Steve that they'd be making one small detour on their way to the airport. When she told him, he didn't look all that happy. "I need to grab a couple of things from my apartment, too, and even more important, stop by the department. Given the nature of what we're doing, I'm not about to leave town without my vest and some other equipment."

Jessie looked at her watch. If traffic was bad across the interstate highway bridge between here and the small airport, they were going to be pushing their luck. Steve seemed to be thinking the same thing.

"I hate to say this, but why don't we split up for the next twenty minutes? I'll forget the apartment and grab my stuff at work and some spare clothes I keep in my locker. You go by your office and get your computer and passport, and I'll meet you there. We'll leave your car in the lot, drop off Maude's stuff at Mom's and be on our way."

"Sounds like a plan." Jessie gave him a brief hug and a kiss on the cheek. "I'll see you there." She dashed back in the house, made sure everything was locked up and exited through the garage. She knew from past experience she could make it to work in five minutes if she took the side streets. In the evening traffic it took more like eight minutes, but soon she was there.

In her haste she almost left the car unlocked as she hurried to the building. Using the remote key she heard the locks shut down and dodged a skateboarding student on the sidewalk.

The offices were as quiet as could be. The full-time tenured instructors left most of the evening classes to part-timers, so the department was abandoned most nights by five. Toward the back she could see the soft glow of a desk lamp in her office, the only light in the hall coming from her slightly open door.

She wondered why Linda hadn't done things the

way she'd told her. The woman was usually so efficient that this came as a surprise. Still, she didn't have enough time to think about it much now. At least the computer was shut down and closed, and the power cord neatly gathered beside it. Sliding both into the leather backpack she used to transport them, Jessie fished her work keys out of her purse and searched for the small one that unlocked her desk drawer. She had just gotten it in the lock when the light went out.

It took a moment for her eyes to adjust to the dark, but when she did she saw motion in a corner. Her heart nearly went through the roof of her mouth. "Who's there? If you move any closer I'm calling nine-one-one."

"There's no need for that," a familiar voice said. "Not that it would work anyway. I took the liberty of disabling your phone before you came back. Once I saw what was on that computer screen and traced your search history back a few screens I knew I had to get you in here. That's a pity, because I really was getting to like you, Jessica."

It was Linda Turner's voice, and yet it wasn't. In the shadows between her desk and the door that was her only escape, Jessie could see the soft glint of metal in Linda's hand. "Wh-what are you talking about?"

"It's clear that you've figured out way too much about my past. Or should I say my past life? It does seem like it was another person who worked as a marshal. And since that person conveniently died in a car accident much like your parents had, it was easy to become someone else."

The woman who stepped from the shadows pointing a gun at Jessie didn't look like the sweet, middle-aged person who'd taken the job as the department secretary. This woman had a hard set to her face, had done away with the reading glasses "Linda" had worn and she looked quite at home with the small automatic in her hand.

"What do you want from me?" If Jessie thought her heart had been racing before, now it threatened to leap from her chest. "Whatever it is, you can take it as long as you just let me out of here. I won't tell anybody. I just want to go find my sister."

"You don't have to leave me to do that, Jessica. I can take you to her even faster than Agent Richards. And perhaps you can even have some kind of touching farewell with her before they sedate you and put you in isolation."

"I don't believe you." Jessie willed her voice not to shake. "You're just bluffing to keep me here for some reason. I know where Laura is, and I know you don't work for the people who have her."

"Oh, no. I don't need to bluff. You see, Jake Brandino and I are going to do each other a favor. It won't be the first time I've done business with him and he pays very well. Only this time we're both coming out ahead because he'll have the means to make his precious boy all better and I won't have to worry about the one person who could identify me. It's so much more lucrative than killing you and making it look like a suicide." As she spoke the woman edged closer to Jessie until there was nothing for her to do but sit down in her desk chair.

Looking up at her from a seated position Jessie's brain went into overdrive to match her heart, and long-suppressed memories slid into place. "I've seen you before. I tried to tell you and a man in a black suit about what I'd seen the night my mother disappeared."

"Yes, and you could have listened to us like a good little girl and believed that you'd imagined it all. If you would have just shut up then Patrick and I could have lived a somewhat normal life."

"After you shot Joshua's father, you mean? With him to take the fall you were home free, weren't you? But then somebody told you about the kid with a weird story, right, Cass?"

The woman's eyes widened in surprise. "Nobody had to tell me. I was Paula's handler. Jake promised me a clean sweep that night, but when it came down to business he couldn't kill little kids. And you were too smart back then, just like you're too smart now."

She motioned with the small, deadly looking weapon. "Get up and get moving, and don't try anything. I promised Jake I'd deliver you alive, but that doesn't necessarily mean I have to get you there in one piece." Grabbing Jessie's arm she applied pressure in a way that made Jessie wince. For once Jessie wished she'd paid more attention to the part-time instructors who taught in the evenings. Then maybe she would know if anyone was in the building who might hear her.

Before she could do anything they were out in the cool night air, exiting through a seldom-used side door. Cassidy had her purse and knew how to open Jessie's car. Reaching into the back of her waistband somewhere she came up with some kind of plastic strap. Pushing Jessie against the side of the car roughly, she spun her around and had the bands around her wrists before Jessie could react.

"Temporary handcuffs. Just one of the cute little things law enforcement came up with in the last twenty years to make my job easier."

Cassidy had the front passenger door of the car open now, and her free hand on the top of Jessie's head, trying to force her down onto the seat. Suddenly all the anger and pain Jessie had bottled up for so many years surged to the surface and she fought back. Even though the woman was in far better shape than she'd pretended to be as Linda Turner, Jessie still had youth on her side. Turning sideways she used her shoulder to plow into Cassidy's chest as hard as she could, rewarded by the satisfying sound of the air whooshing out of her lungs as she fell back.

Jessie ran and dodged between the few cars on the lot, feeling like an easy target. It was still hard for her to pray and do anything else at the same time, but she pleaded silently for help as she ducked around a pickup truck. When a familiar car came to a quick stop nearby she almost sobbed with relief. But her relief was short-lived as Steve jumped out of the car, right under one of the parking lot lights.

"Steve, watch out. She's got a gun," Jessie shrieked even as she tried to get even lower behind the pickup truck. She could hear the sound of running feet, then a pop and the driver's side window of the truck dissolved into thousands of pieces.

"Stop now. I've got backup on the way," Steve barked from his position behind the driver's side door of his car where he'd taken refuge. "Jessie, are you okay?"

"Yes. I'm fine." Jessie thought she could feel gritty pebbles of glass in her hair, and her ears were ringing but otherwise she was okay. Ten yards away the door to her car slammed, and the engine started at almost the same moment. With a squeal of brakes the car tore out of the lot, headlights out.

Steve rushed to where she sat on the pavement and started looking her over. "Aren't you afraid she'll get away?" Jessie asked, trying to get up.

"Let her go. I can radio in the information on your car and somebody else can go after her. Right now I want to make sure you're really okay, and tell Richards what just happened." He helped her into a standing position with shaking hands, and didn't let go once he got her steady. "What did just happen, anyway? When you didn't call me once you picked up your stuff I began to get nervous. I got over here quickly just in time to see you come out that door with a gun at your back. I think my heart about stopped."

"I'm glad it didn't. I'd hug you but I've got a little problem." Jessie motioned with her cuffed wrists. "I hope there's a simple way to get these things off, because I don't want to wear them all the way to the airport."

Steve started shaking his head. "Oh, no. You can't believe that after all of this we're going to Canada tonight."

Jessie knew she must look a little deranged with

her straggly hair, glasses askew and pebbles of windshield probably caught in her hair, as well. "Stephen, I can't believe anything else. Once you give the shortest possible report to whoever answers this call from your department, I'm getting to Spirit of St. Louis even if I have to hitchhike."

"Then let me get you out of those things while we wait for the deputies. While I find my pocketknife, lean over and shake your head, gently. I don't want you to cut yourself."

Doing what he told her, Jessie thought those might have been the loveliest words Steve had said to her in days. Let other women have men who whispered sweet nothings in their ears. Steve was going against his every instinct to let her find her sister, and if that wasn't love Jessie didn't know what was.

Later, on the small, fast jet to Canada, Steve found a blanket somewhere, and a comb and made her lean forward while he gently went through all her hair searching for errant glass. "I don't know which one of us is crazier," Joshua Richards muttered. "You for still wanting to come or Gardner here for agreeing to it or me for not stopping the whole operation after what happened back there."

"Probably you," Jessie heard Steve say. "But then you haven't known this woman as long as I have.

Give her a couple more weeks and you'll realize that we couldn't have stopped her from doing this unless Cassidy had actually shot her in that parking lot."

Jessie, her head turned toward Joshua while Steve combed through the last of her hair, saw an enigmatic look cross the agent's face. *Somebody shot Cassidy*, she thought but didn't say anything. The knowledge was more than she could handle tonight, so she stayed silent. A few minutes later she agreed with Steve's suggestion that she recline her seat and try to get some rest, even though she knew she wasn't likely to. Much later she woke up still clutching his arm as the dark sky passed by outside the windows of the plane while a row in front of them Joshua Richards looked out into the blackness, a look of grim determination etched on his face. This time prayer came easily for Jessie as she silently asked her newfound Father to keep them all in His care.

FIFTEEN

"No matter what happens, you will not leave this van." Joshua Richards accentuated every word, his steel-blue eyes like lasers on Jessie's face. "Are we perfectly clear about that?"

"We are." Jessie settled into the captain's chair in the back of what looked like a panel truck. "I didn't come all this way to mess anything up, believe me."

"I appreciate that. And I'm grateful for the information you were able to pass on after the incident last night with Cassidy. We have a team going through the offices in your institution's history department to try and learn all that we can about her."

Jessie narrowed her eyes. "Does this mean she's not dead after all? Earlier on the plane I saw a look from you that made me wonder if she'd been shot."

"We think she was shot, but not fatally. She ditched your car after a chase and it was found with blood in the front seat, but not enough to make anyone think she was dead."

Jessie shuddered. "Am I supposed to drive that car again?"

Joshua grimaced. "Probably not. At the least I'll make sure that the bureau pays for taking out the seats and replacing them, not just a thorough cleaning. Besides, we need to go over those front seats with a fine-tooth comb anyway. She wasn't in this alone and her partner's still out there somewhere."

Jessie finally asked something that had been on her mind for hours. "How do we know that there will be anybody at the clinic anyway? With as much time as she had to warn people, won't they have taken Laura and Adrian to another location?"

"They would have if they'd gotten any messages. Reception from cell phones and Internet service providers is so bad in this area surrounding the clinic that no one would think it odd to go twelve hours without messages from those sources. Naturally we made the extra effort to assure that any messages that might have gotten in were blocked or the normal frequencies were jammed."

Jessie thought that was a brilliant idea and said so. Meanwhile the team assembling to rush the clinic was loading up weapons, checking each other's bulletproof gear and double-checking every-thing. Still, if she were the one putting on body armor and running up to a place as remote as this one, defended by known gangsters, maybe she'd try to convince herself it was safe, too. It was bad enough to be left behind here knowing Steve would be going into this dangerous situation.

Then he was in front of her, and she shivered a little to see him in all the protective gear, carrying weapons like the rest. She had known all along that his job was dangerous and he carried a gun any time he was on duty, but this brought it all home in a dif-ferent way. "Be careful out there," she said softly, putting her hands on his shoulders. "Don't get too heroic for your own good, okay?"

"I won't. I've got too much to lose to try foolish heroics. Keep praying for me while we're doing this. And say a few for Joshua and the rest of the crew."

"For everyone," she said softly. Reaching up on tiptoe, she gave him a quick kiss on the cheek. "I'll see you back here soon." Watching him head off with the others, the lump in her throat felt like an orange. Laura wondered what this growing aware-ness of faith would be like once all the excitement was over. Could she sustain this belief when there wasn't anything to worry about? Right now hope was a life preserver in the tossing sea of emotions all around her. When the waves calmed down, where would that leave her? It wasn't a question she could answer.

Four in the morning had never been Steve's favorite time of day. Too late to be night, too early to feel like morning, it was disjointed and more eerie than peaceful. The darkness that had been velvety black a few hours before now thinned out to a deep gray. Adding this discomfort to the hot, chafing body armor and the unaccustomed weight of the weapons he carried made him hyperaware of the situation they all faced. There weren't enough prayers available to keep him truly calm as he faced this task.

The tiny radio unit in his right ear came to life with Joshua's voice. "All positions set. Ram team in place to move in ninety seconds. Alpha unit, you call the shots from here on out."

"Roger that" came another deep voice Steve knew belonged to Rick, the coordinator of the RCMP special tactical squad with the battering ram and the five-person team that would rush the medical facility right behind the ram. Normally their expertise was in getting into drug labs, but this operation had enough similarity to a drug raid that Rick was in charge.

The ninety seconds until the final rush dragged by interminably. Even though Steve could see team members slip into place with precision it still felt as if it was all taking forever. Then finally the woods exploded with noise from flash grenades and the sound of the ram on the heavy door of the clinic. Alarms sounded from inside as the team rushed the building, with the American contingent only seconds behind them.

Incredibly they reached the heart of the clinic with little, if any bloodshed. The shocked medical personnel were whisked outside except for a few key people needed to open doors and direct the teams to the patients they sought. By now the building's power had been cut and what lights were left came from a generator, dimming the corridors and the nurses' station at their hub.

Steve raced along behind Rick and the rest of a four-person team navigating the corridors until they came to a large room hung with sterile drapes pulled back from the glass wall that made up the front of the room. Framed by the yellow drapes was a figure on a bed, her breathing so shallow she looked like an animated Sleeping Beauty. Blond hair poured over the pillow and one thin wrist and delicate hand drooped from the confines of the railed hospital bed. "Is that her?" Rick asked. Steve nodded, recognizing Laura from the pictures he'd seen and the memory of the bedside vigil at another hospital.

"That's her." He understood now why even Jessie had been fooled into thinking that the person they'd watched dying was Laura. The bone structure, the hair and even the way she lay on the bed were the same as her mother. This woman, however had not been ravaged by fire and violence so her porcelain skin was unnaturally pale but otherwise untouched.

"There's one other confirmation…can I go in there to check something out, or will it harm her?"

Rick shrugged. "We're going to need to take her out of the room eventually. The guy next door, too. How we're supposed to get somebody from special ops germ-free enough to do that is beyond me."

To be as safe as he possibly could, Steve went to a nearby station and scrubbed his hands, put on one of the masks there and sterile gloves. Then he opened the door and went into the small room where Laura lay on the bed. She appeared to be dressed in hospital scrubs and Steve lifted the sheet covering her feet and legs. There on her ankle was the one thing that he was looking for; a tiny tattoo of a bluebird. "Jessie is going to be so happy," he said to her, even though he doubted she could hear him. He settled the sheet back in position and walked out of the room, not wanting to risk contaminating her anymore with his outside germs.

Personnel still milled around the main rooms of

the clinic. "Looks like we got an added bonus," Rick crowed, pointing to the entrance where three team members clustered around a dark-haired man in khaki pants and a silk sweater. "The man himself was paying a little visit to the clinic. It seems that the last message that made it through was one from somebody with the information that they'd gotten hold of Jessie so there was fresh blood available."

Jake Brandino seemed unruffled by everything. He probably thought that like most other situations, some high-priced lawyer he had on retainer would get him out of this one. From all the setup work Richards had done, even Steve knew that wasn't going to be the case. He wished he could stick around to see the fireworks when Brandino found out otherwise.

"Mission accomplished," Richards said, coming up beside him. "Looks like you're already set to be part of the crew that gets these two to the waiting rescue units." He nodded toward Laura and the unseen figure in the room next to her.

"It would be my pleasure, provided that somewhere along the way Jessie gets to have a minute with her sister."

"She kept her promise, and I'll keep mine. I don't know what kind of prep the medical staff will make her do, but no matter what they say I'm going to push for her to be there. In fact, if I can swing it she'll go in the helicopter that takes Laura on the first leg of the journey to a clinic in the States."

"I'm beginning to like you after all," Steve said to Joshua, who finally cracked a smile.

"Great. And I didn't even have to take a bullet to make that happen."

Thursday. Seattle, Washington

Contrasting this hospital vigil with the one just a few weeks ago, Jessie was overwhelmed by the differences. The first time around death had been a foregone conclusion. Now it still hovered as a threat, but the doctors had tried to assure them all that Laura, at least, would be all right once her immune system got a little stronger.

Adrian's outlook remained guarded, and Jessie wished there was some way closer than the communication port in the glass that made up the front of his "clean room" environment for her to communicate with him. They couldn't pass photos back and forth, touch each other or share other mementos that couldn't be sterilized. "We've got twenty-four years to catch up on, and who knows how much time to do it," he complained. "I'm tempted to ignore them all and just walk out of here, Jessie. It's my fault that

Laura's as bad off as she is, and I can't think of a way to make it up to her."

"You certainly wouldn't do her any good if you came out of there," Jessie snapped. "And your testimony is going to be the key to taking down the whole Brandino organization...." She trailed off when she thought about her brother's feelings. "I'm sorry. That's easy for me to say, but I imagine it's difficult for you to think of your uncle as the enemy."

"Not anymore. I always felt like there was something more than the life he groomed me to lead, something else I was supposed to be doing instead. And once I found out that I had another family someplace else that nobody ever bothered to tell me about, I lost the last respect I had for him."

There was a look of longing and pain on his drawn young face, and Jessie put her hand up to the glass, the closest she could get to comforting him. His brow scrunched up and he blurted a question. "Do you think he ordered Mom's death?"

Jessie weighed her reply for a moment. "Not anymore. Although he wouldn't have been too heartbroken to get rid of her by that point, some of your neighbors in the town house complex recognized pictures of Cassidy as being somebody who slipped in and out of the building that day." Jessie had filled Adrian in on all the things that happened in and around his apartment once he'd been taken away, and told him about her department secretary who turned out to be a totally different person than she claimed.

The former marshal had vanished again, leaving everyone to wonder where she and her partner might turn up next. Jessie knew that Joshua hoped the two were gone for good, spirited away someplace out of the country to live off their ill-gotten gains. Jessie wasn't so sure she could believe that. Cassidy seemed to enjoy vengeance too much to let anything go. Still, there were now too many cases piling up against her and the mysterious Patrick to allow them to come out of hiding for long. One slip and they'd be on trial for federal crimes.

Jessie wasn't sure how to give Adrian the one piece of news she had today. It wasn't in her nature to beat around the bush, so she just came out with it. "I'm going to be out of commission for a few days starting on Monday. Maybe by then they'll have the bugs worked out of that computer system they've been promising you. That way we could still talk, or at least e-mail and IM."

He gave her a wary look. "This doesn't have anything to do with that bright purple pressure wrap around your arm yesterday does it? You told me that was for donating platelets. For Laura."

"Hey, I donated platelets and they did go to Laura. But I gave blood for some lab work too and it looks like I'm an even better match for you than Laura. It's not like anybody could get me out of here anyway. Until the two of you are ready to walk out of here on your own, I'm staying, too. I might as well make myself useful." She tried to sound braver than she felt about the whole process of having doctors harvest bone marrow and stem cells to give to Adrian.

His face clouded, changing the color of his blue-gray eyes to something stormier. "What if I told you not to do it?"

"I'd treat you the same way I would Laura if she was the one with a life-threatening illness. I'd thank you for your love and concern and go ahead and do exactly what I felt was right." Just saying the words made Jessie sure they were the truth. She was beginning to understand what Steve meant when he said he'd been "led" to certain decisions by his faith. A sense of being drawn to the right and the good seemed to grow in her as she became more comfortable with being a Christian.

"Yeah, well, I still don't like it." Adrian looked down and his lower lip stuck out.

Jessie couldn't help laughing a little. "Brother, dear, right now you look just like what you are…a kid the age of most of my students back in St. Charles. At least give me some credit for knowledge I might have picked up in the seven years or so I've got on you, huh?"

"Maybe. It still doesn't sound right that you'd risk your life for me when you don't even really know me yet. What kind of person does that?"

Jessie's heart sang. "Have I got a story for you," she said. Was it too soon to start telling him about the Friend she had just come to know? Maybe he knew a little bit already and this was her opportunity to tell him more. She took a deep breath and tried to figure out where to begin.

Steve stood by a nurses' station where he could watch the interaction between Jessie and her brother. He'd never heard her laugh like that before, never seen her show so much lightheartedness. When she stretched her fingers out on the pane of glass and Adrian mirrored her, Steve nearly turned and walked away. He'd wondered before what would happen to his growing relationship with Jessie once they found Laura. Now he knew. The last few days he felt more and more removed from Jessie with each passing hour.

In a way it might even be worse now that Jessie had *two* siblings to be with, bond with and enjoy.

Whatever they were talking about, both she and Adrian looked happy. Watching Jessie there Steve came to a decision he'd been mulling over for a day and a half. It was time to cut his losses and move on. He crossed the distance between them and put his hand on her shoulder. "We need to talk. I have to go back home."

She looked at him, then back to her brother. Adrian waved her toward Steve. "Go talk to the man, Jessie. I'll still be here when you're done."

"That's true. For now I have a captive audience with you." Jessie gave her brother a teasing smile and followed Steve into a small family conference room nearby. "Okay, tell me all about this. How long do you think you'll be gone? And will you bring Maude back with you? I miss her something fierce."

Great. Now he'd been demoted to dog courier. If Steve had felt left out before, this was a new low. What would she do with the dog anyway? There was no way they'd let her come to this specialized hospital setting. "What would you do with her all day?"

"She could stay in my apartment. There's room." Jessie had a studio at a nearby building that catered to the families of patients in this specialized cancer hospital. He'd seen the inside of the place once and even though it was a little Spartan, it looked okay.

It didn't strike him as the perfect place to leave a dog all day and he almost said so. Then he thought better of that and kept his mouth shut, hoping she'd say something else.

When instead she just smiled up at him expectantly, Steve pushed ahead with what he had to do. "No, you don't understand, Jess. I have to go home for good. St. Charles is still where I belong and I've got to go back and do the job they pay me to do. The FBI isn't offering me the kind of protective custody they're giving you and Laura and Adrian."

All the sparkle left Jessie's eyes and her smile disappeared. "Oh. But I thought you'd stay here awhile. At least until I got all prepped and had my surgery."

That was another issue he didn't particularly want to get into with Jessie. He wasn't sure of the wisdom of doing this for Adrian, who was still a total stranger in a lot of ways. He'd seen enough of Jessie's determination to know not to argue with her so he didn't try. "I can't do that. Like I said, I have a job to do back there. I've already been away from the department long enough I'm probably out of the rotation on major crimes. There's got to be mail waist high from the slot in the front door of my apartment, and I need to get back to my regular life."

Tell me none of that matters, he willed her

silently. *Say you love me and you need me here. Say anything that would convince me to stay.*

Instead her expression got somber and her chin stuck out with determination. "I'm sorry, Steve." She kept an even, measured tone, not something you'd use with a guy you just couldn't live without. "Right now I belong here."

"I thought that's what you'd say." He leaned down and kissed her cheek, feeling the rose-petal softness of her skin in contrast to his, which hadn't seen a razor for a day and a half. "I'll be back in tomorrow before I take off for the airport." *If I can manage to walk out right now without making the world's biggest fool of myself,* he added silently before he turned and walked away. He strained his ears the length of the hospital corridor, but Jessie didn't say anything that would have called him back to her or made him change his mind.

SIXTEEN

"You can't go back to St. Louis." Joshua Richards stood in front of Jessie, arms crossed over his chest, shaking his head. "At least not now and not alone like you want to. It's just not going to be part of our deal."

"I already regret I made that deal," Jessie grumbled.

"Only because it's interfering with your love life. Otherwise you're as anxious to see Jake Brandino brought to justice as I am. And you know that your testimony, along with Laura's and Adrian's will be what puts him away."

"If I'd known that having the FBI protect us would be almost as bad as the witness protection program I might have thought twice." Jessie tried to make her posture as tough as her words, and stifled a groan. She felt worn-out and sick to her stomach from the general anesthesia they'd used. All the places where she'd had needles poked in her, lines taped to her skin and technicians probing for one more place to find a spot for some piece of equipment clamored for first place on her personal list of sore spots.

None of them could compete with the bone-deep ache in her hip where they'd taken out bone marrow. The nurses had told her that each donor had a different reaction to the removal, and lucky her, she was about the sorest they'd ever seen. Normally she hated painkillers, choosing not to use them because of the lack of control she felt while on them. But today she blessed whoever invented the medications that allowed her to be propped up in bed without wanting to scream.

While the pain medication dulled the physical aches, nothing much touched the ache in her heart. She really expected to hear from Stephen by now, but it hadn't happened. Going through the preparation and the surgery without him made her feel empty. She hadn't realized just how deep a part of her life he'd become until he wasn't there anymore. What had the last two months meant to him? Now that the investigation was over, did it mean their relationship was finished, too?

She lay back against the pillows letting sadness wash over her. Life was finally coming together in so many ways, yet she had no one to share it with in the way she wanted. Steve had protected her, encouraged her and shown her an entire new way of life. And then he left. "Steve's testimony is going to be important, too. I hope you're protecting him as well as you're protecting us."

Joshua scowled a little. "He's a detective with a large law enforcement agency. We're doing what we can, or at least what he'll let us do. But you don't have the training and resources that he does, Ms. Barker. That's the biggest reason that I can't agree to any quick trips back to Missouri for you. Anyplace you go for a while you're going to require protection."

Jessie sighed. "Just call me by my first name. We're going to be involved in this whole effort to convict Brandino for long enough that formality might as well go out the window."

"Maybe for you. I need to do my job, even when it doesn't make me very popular. That includes keeping the three of you as safe as possible before, during and after any hearings involving Jake Brandino and the crime family he's a part of."

Jessie tried to keep her temper in check. She owed Joshua Richards and his task force a great deal for bringing her back together with Laura. And he wasn't responsible for her happiness, just her safety. "I'm sorry, Agent Richards. It's difficult for me to admit you're right, but you are. Letting someone else be in charge is difficult for me."

The man seemed taken aback by her admission. "Hey, isn't this argument supposed to go on for a while? I haven't won one this easily in months, especially not with you." Now it was Jessie's turn to be surprised.

"Okay, you got me. I didn't know you were capable of making a joke, or smiling." Even his steel-blue eyes warmed up when he smiled all the way. "But then I guess I haven't given you much occasion to smile, have I?"

"Don't feel bad about that, Ms. Barker. In that respect I have to give you credit because you've given me the biggest reason to smile that I've had in years. As bad as it was otherwise, your encounter with Cassidy made it possible to clear my father's name." There was a peaceful quality to Joshua as he said the words. Jessie wondered for a moment what he'd do now that his personal mission was done. But it wasn't her place to ask, so she kept quiet.

Joshua finally sat down in the chair next to Jessie's bed, a move that filled her with relief. He looked so keyed up standing by the window. Maybe now he'd be still for a moment. "So explain to me why you want so badly to go back home right away. You know we've promised to help you move in just a few weeks."

"Throwing in a false information trail about where we're going, as well, and all at no cost," Jessie said, trying not to sound as snide as she felt. "At least I don't have much in the way of family and friends who will be confused when their Christmas cards come back."

"Hey, be glad I was able to get those higher than me to agree to this unusual situation. Only the fact that you wouldn't have anything to do with the federal marshals kept my bosses from turning everything over to them and Homeland Security where it should have gone."

"I know, and really, I'm thankful for that part. It could have been a lot worse."

"Anything with my sister involved could have been a lot worse, Agent Richards," a cheery voice called from the doorway. Laura breezed into the room as fast as she was able. With each day she looked more like her old self, although Jessie's room was close enough to hers to realize that Laura's nights brought restless sleep and nightmares.

"Well, you must be feeling better because you're getting obnoxious," Jessie said, unable to stay unhappy around Laura. "Thanks for coming by to see me. This is a change, me in bed and you up and around."

Laura grinned, making her blue eyes light up. "I'm enjoying being more mobile again. Now we need to get us both that way at the same time. Maybe we can check out the local malls."

Joshua shook his head. "And I thought your sister was the hard one to corral. You're going to be interesting, Laura."

"Hey, what happened to formality?"

The agent shrugged. "I can't call you both 'Ms. Barker' without beginning to sound positively Victorian. So you're going to get your way for that, at least. And since you have somebody else to keep you company, I'm going to head out for a while. I need to talk to your brother anyway."

Laura come closer to the bedside and took the chair Richards had vacated. "Go on. He's having a good day and he'd welcome the company. I think I was starting to bore him."

"I doubt that," Jessie told her sister as the agent left. "It's hard to imagine you boring anybody. Are you really feeling as good as you look?"

"I think I am. Are you as uncomfortable as you sound?" Laura's face showed concern.

"I didn't think it showed, but I'm not all that great. I guess I'm just crabby and lonely and anxious for all of this to be over so I can find a way to get that man to let me travel."

"He's just trying to keep us safe, Jess. After what happened with me, that sounds like a really good idea." She leaned back in her chair and pulled one heel up on the seat, wrapping her arms around her leg. It was Laura's thoughtful position, one that Jessie could never figure out how she managed. "Hmm. Maybe if we could find the right team to be the bodyguards, or whatever they're going to call them, then he'd be willing to cut us a little slack."

"Maybe." She hated to squash Laura's idea, but she didn't feel as hopeful about that as her sister. Jessie knew the bodyguard she'd want most, and he wasn't available for the job.

She didn't realize the pain medication was taking effect until Laura spoke softly to her a few minutes later. "Looks like you're drifting off. I'll go see what I can do about that bodyguard problem while you take a nap."

"Fine," Jessie agreed. Today wasn't the day for arguments with Laura. There might never be a day for arguments with her sister again, now that she was back and life with her seemed so very precious.

"This is a temporary setback," Jessie muttered through teeth clenched to stop their chattering. Two days after she'd donated bone marrow for Adrian, about the time most people were feeling just fine and bopping around the halls according to the nurses, she got to be the one-in-a-hundred with an infection afterward. Antibiotics dripped from the bag on a pole over her left hand while she fought alternating bouts of fever and chills.

Laura had been banished from the room unless she scrubbed down and wore a mask and other protective clothing. When Jessie heard that, she virtually ordered her sister to stay away. "There's no sense in two of us getting sick. The doctors will skin me if they think I've passed on whatever germ this is to you."

Laura had agreed, still a bit teary and pouting, but not arguing. There seemed to be something on her mind that she wasn't sharing with Jessie. No matter what she asked Laura about Adrian's condition and any developments in the case, her reply had been the same: "You don't need to worry about any of that right now. Just get better." Of course that didn't help much.

So here she was during sleepless night number two, waiting for the medicines the doctors were pumping into her to have their desired effects. The modern-language Bible she'd had one of the nurses find for her and bring in was her best source of comfort right now, reminding her that she wasn't really alone in all this.

As if to reassure her another nurse came into the

room just then, not bothering to turn on the light or make much noise. Quietly and efficiently the woman looked at the bag of fluid on the pole, removed a vial from one of her pockets and started to attach it to the port in the bag. Jessie felt a little puzzled by her actions. Hadn't someone just changed the bag about an hour before? She tried to see the clock in the darkened room. Maybe she'd slept more than she thought and it was time for this to happen again. In any case she didn't remember anyone else mixing solutions as this woman seemed to be doing.

As she started to ask the nurse about that Jessie heard the soft whoosh of the elevator doors at the end of the hall, followed by quick, heavy footfalls and an odd clicking noise. Somewhere in the recesses of her foggy brain she searched for what could be making that sound. It was familiar, but she couldn't quite place it. There was a large shadow in the doorway, making the nurse turn toward the figure. "You can't bring that in here," she said in a quiet but officious tone. "Don't you have any idea how dangerous that is? I'm calling security."

"Hey, I'm sorry," said a deep male voice, which rose a little louder as the whole shadow loomed forward. Then there was a low growling sound and then a flurry of action all at once.

The nurse cried out as if in pain while the man raised his voice. "No! What's gotten into you? You're going to get us all in trouble." He pulled back to the doorway and Jessie could see him groping for the light switch. He reached it just about the same time Jessie found the control on the bed rail that turned on the lamp over her head.

For a moment the light dazed her and then she felt sure she was hallucinating when she looked at the figures struggling near the door. Then the site where the needle went into the top of her left hand began to burn and taking her eyes off the trio just inside the room she ripped off the tape holding it steady and plucked it out. Clamping her thumb down on the place where blood now dripped she groped clumsily for the call button while yelling for help. "Call security and the police!" she shouted, trying to lower one of the bed rails so that she could get out of the high bed. "Anybody, we need help. Call the police!"

Before she could say more the man slammed the small figure in nurse's scrubs into the wall. "It's going to be okay. I've got her. Did she hurt you, Jess?"

"I don't know. It depends on what she put in that bag." Steve pulled out a cell phone and started talking into it while keeping his left arm stiff against the throat of the struggling woman. "We need police up here as soon as possible, and the emergency room staff all on the third floor transplant suite. Now."

Breaking off the call, he nearly roared his yells for help out into the hall where one lone aide finally came down the corridor at a run. "Check the other two rooms and make sure they're okay. This woman I'm holding isn't a nurse and she may have tried to kill your patients."

The next person in scrubs Steve directed over to Jessie's bedside and the wide-eyed young intern checked her over quickly, put pressure over the spot where she'd removed the needle and tried to read the label on the bag now dripping fluid onto the floor. "Are you short of breath? Heart pounding? Any more severe pain anyplace?" he asked Jessie while at the same time she felt something land on the bed.

"I think I'm all right. And don't you dare try to take this dog off the bed," she warned the intern. "No matter what else happens, she's not moving."

"Sure. Fine," he said, too busy working on her hand to quibble about Maude licking her face in happy abandon.

In less than two minutes the room was a swarm of security personnel and Seattle police officers as well as at least one man Jessie recognized as one of Joshua Richards's specially picked staff. Cassidy had been cuffed and whisked out of the room. Once Steve didn't have to hold on to her anymore he was at Jessie's side instantly. Before either of them said anything he leaned over and gave her a long, fervent kiss. After the interruption with Maude, the intern finishing up on Jessie's hand didn't even give them a second glance.

"Are you sure you're okay?" Steve's worried eyes searched her face.

"If that vial contains what it says it does, she should be all right," the intern said, wrapping the last of a bandage. "It's concentrated potassium solution. A little bit of it in the IV line wouldn't be so bad. But if everything she pushed in there had gone into your body, you would have died within twenty minutes or so." He looked hard at Jessie and then at Steve. "You got really lucky there."

"Not lucky," Jessie said firmly. "Blessed. Incredibly blessed."

There was more commotion at the door and Laura burst into the room. "Steve! What went on in here? And how did you sneak the dog in? Come here, sweetie." Maude jumped off the bed and dashed over to Laura, deciding she was okay and giving her a quick kiss, then going back to Jessie on the bed, all at a speed Jessie didn't think was possible on those short, stubby legs.

"You're okay." Relief washed over Jessie at the sight of her sister with tousled hair and pajamas, but looking fine otherwise. "How's Adrian?"

"Fine. Asleep until all of this commotion. Whatever happened, they went for you first."

"Fortunately, so did Steve and Maude." She looked up into Steve's eyes, their green and brown depths radiating love. "Now they'll probably be back in here hooking me up to more antibiotics in a little while, and they'll try to shoo everybody out. But no matter what they say, we're all staying in here for the rest of the night."

"Yes, we are. I'll help you argue for anything you want," Steve said, holding her free hand.

"Me, too," Laura said. "Even if I have to sleep sitting up on a chair, I'm not leaving until after sunrise."

Neither the medical staff nor Joshua Richards had been successful in getting Steve and Laura or even Maude out of Jessie's room. The four of them had held firm to the point of wheeling in a recliner for Laura to sleep in, where Maude had finally joined her after being coaxed off the bed by Steve.

In the early-morning hours once Jessie had been thoroughly looked over by her doctors and the room was quiet again, she and Steve talked softly, heads together so they didn't wake Laura or the snoozing dog. "How much of a part did my sister play in getting you back out here?"

Steve chuckled. "About equal with my mother. Laura told me you looked miserable without me, and Mom told me I was an idiot for coming back alone. It didn't take long for me to admit she was right."

"I have a lot to thank Laura for. If she hadn't coaxed you to come back the way she did, you wouldn't have been here when Cassidy slipped into my room."

"Joshua said it wasn't the first time she'd been on the floor. He told me the doctors think now that your infection might have been caused by her, just so you'd have an IV line she could tamper with. She could have been in and out of here so quickly no one would ever have known why you died." Jessie could feel him shudder. She put her unencumbered hand on his shoulder.

"That wasn't the way God wanted it to be for us. This may all look like a great string of coincidences to some people here, but I don't think so. After this I'm willing to trust His timetable for my life."

"Good. I hope you think it includes me because this time I'm not leaving. I want to stay by you and protect you as long as you need the protection, Jessie. I want to get to know your sister and your brother. I love you, and I want to make you a permanent part of my life, no matter what kind of adjustments it means we'll both have to make."

"We've got as long as we need to talk about that, Stephen. With God to guide us, I'm sure we'll get through whatever happens. Together."

That was the way the dietary aide found the group when she brought in Jessie's breakfast tray. All four of the room's occupants slept, smiles on their faces. She set down the tray on the bedside table and went away quietly, knowing that when her family met at the dinner table that evening, she would definitely win their daily contest for the oddest thing that happened in their day. This one would be the highlight of the week, she thought, walking up the hall with a smile even bigger than the dog's.

* * * * *

Dear Reader,

Sometimes writers have stories that take hold and won't let go, and *To Trust a Stranger* was one of those for me. I've carried Jessie and Laura's story around in my head for a while now and finally got the chance to put it down on paper.

As I write this, it's just a little later in the year than their story takes place, and Missouri has already had a couple of rounds of ice and snow. While I miss the people and places of my "home state" I have to admit that I do enjoy the weather here in my current home in Southern California. Whatever the weather is doing this fall where you are, I hope you are entertained and uplifted by Jessie's story and it reminds you of who you are and Whose you are.

Blessings,

Lynn Bulock

QUESTIONS FOR DISCUSSION

1. Did you ever tell a story as a child that no one would believe? What did it feel like?

2. People who enter the Witness Security program have to assume their new identity without telling anyone from their old life goodbye. Who would be the hardest person in your life to leave? Why?

3. Jessica and Laura's mother chose one part of her family over another. Why do you think she made the choice she did?

4. Working in law enforcement, Steve can't always witness to his faith by words. What kinds of actions did he perform that showed he was a Christian?

5. Have you ever been in a place where you couldn't witness by words but wanted to tell someone else about your faith? What did you do?

6. Read Psalm 91 together. What might have been happening to and around the writer at the time this psalm was being written? How can you relate to that?

7. Joshua's purpose in life is to get revenge or vindication. What do you think he will do when that motive is gone?

8. Some of the characters in this book seem to put their trust in "other Gods" or let other things rule their lives. Why doesn't this work?

9. Kyra's actions spoke as loudly as the cross she wore around her neck. Have you ever met anyone whose jewelry or clothing proclaimed them to be Christian, but their actions said something else? How did you react?

10. Adrian's only real chance for survival is a bone marrow transplant from someone else. Who would you do that for? Who would do it for you?

Love Inspired®

Celebrate Love Inspired's 10th anniversary with top authors and great stories all year long!

LITTLE MISS MATCHMAKER

BY

DANA CORBIT

A Tiny Blessings Tale

Loving families and needy children continue to come together to fulfill God's greatest plans!

Alex Donovan may be able to fight fires, but he is defenseless against his young niece and her matchmaking plans!

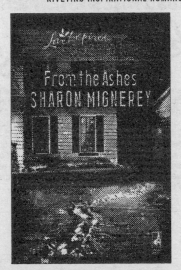

REQUEST YOUR FREE BOOKS!
2 FREE RIVETING INSPIRATIONAL NOVELS PLUS 2 FREE MYSTERY GIFTS

Love Inspired®
SUSPENSE

YES! Please send me 2 FREE Love Inspired® Suspense novels and my 2 FREE mystery gifts. After receiving them, if I don't wish to receive any more books, I can return the shipping statement marked "cancel." If I don't cancel, I will receive 4 brand-new novels every month and be billed just $3.99 per book in the U.S. or $4.74 per book in Canada, plus 25¢ shipping and handling per book and applicable taxes, if any*. That's a savings of 20% off the cover price! I understand that accepting the 2 free books and gifts places me under no obligation to buy anything. I can always return a shipment and cancel at any time. Even if I never buy another book from Steeple Hill, the two free books and gifts are mine to keep forever.

123 IDN EL5H 323 IDN ELQH

Name	(PLEASE PRINT)	
Address		Apt. #
City	State/Prov.	Zip/Postal Code

Signature (if under 18, a parent or guardian must sign)

Order online at www.LoveInspiredSuspense.com

Or mail to Steeple Hill Reader Service™:

IN U.S.A.: P.O. Box 1867, Buffalo, NY 14240-1867
IN CANADA: P.O. Box 609, Fort Erie, Ontario L2A 5X3

Not valid to current Love Inspired Suspense subscribers.

Want to try two free books from another series?
Call 1-800-873-8635 or visit www.morefreebooks.com

* Terms and prices subject to change without notice. NY residents add applicable sales tax. Canadian residents will be charged applicable provincial taxes and GST. This offer is limited to one order per household. All orders subject to approval. Credit or debit balances in a customer's account(s) may be offset by any other outstanding balance owed by or to the customer. Please allow 4 to 6 weeks for delivery.

Your Privacy: Steeple Hill is committed to protecting your privacy. Our Privacy Policy is available online at www.eHarlequin.com or upon request from the Reader Service. From time to time we make our lists of customers available to reputable firms who may have a product or service of interest to you. If you would prefer we not share your name and address, please check here. ☐

Love Inspired®
SUSPENSE

TITLES AVAILABLE NEXT MONTH

Don't miss these four stories in October

SHADOWS IN THE MIRROR by Linda Hall
Her aunt warned her against returning to Burlington,
but Marylee Simson had to know why her parents' very
existence seemed shrouded in mystery...and whether
handsome Evan Baxter could be linked to the tragic accident
that had claimed them.

BURIED SECRETS by Margaret Daley
Fresh from her grandfather's funeral, Maggie Somers
was stunned to find his home ransacked and her family's
nemesis, Zach Collier, amid the wreckage. Could she believe
his warning that the thieves would certainly target her next?

FROM THE ASHES by Sharon Mignerey
Angela London was haunted by her dark past. Now a guide-
dog trainer working with former football star Brian Ramsey,
she needed to thwart a vengeful enemy to protect her
newfound happiness.

BAYOU JUSTICE by Robin Caroll
With an angry past dividing their families, CoCo LeBlanc's
discovery of her former fiancé's father's body in the bayou
put her name at the top of the suspect list. Working with her
ex to clear both their names, could she survive the Cajun
killer's next attack?

LISCNM0907